The Mystery
of the
SMASHING
GLASS

A police lieutenant climbed out of the patrol car.

"All right," he said to the Three Investigators, "you want to tell us why you've been smashing car windows?"

Pete gulped. "We—we didn't break any windows!"

Bob cried, "We're here to catch the window smasher ourselves! We're detectives!"

"You are making a grave mistake," Jupiter said angrily. "If you will look at our credentials—" He reached toward his pocket.

All the policemen came to attention, touching their pistols.

"Hold it right there!" said the lieutenant, and Jupiter froze.

How were the Three Investigators going to get out of this one?

The Three Investigators in

The Mystery
of the
SMASHING
GLASS

by William Arden

Based on characters created by Robert Arthur

Random House   New York

Library of Congress Cataloging in Publication Data:

Arden, William.
   The Three Investigators in
The mystery of the smashing glass.
   (The Three Investigators mystery series ; 38)
   SUMMARY: Three young detectives try to trap an invisible vandal who has
been breaking car windows all over town.
   [1. Mystery and detective stories] I. Arthur, Robert. II. Title. III. Title:
Mystery of the smashing glass. IV. Series.
PZ7.A6794Tl 1984   [Fic]   83-26984
ISBN: 0-394-86550-2 (pbk.); 0-394-96550-7 (lib. bdg.)

Manufactured in the United States of America
   2   3   4   5   6   7   8   9   0

Contents

A Greeting from Hector Sebastian   vii

1. Broken Windows   1
2. The Unseen Force   7
3. The Scene of the Crime   14
4. Alarm!   23
5. Menace in the Junkyard   30
6. Jupiter Finds an M.O.   41
7. Accused!   45
8. A Stolen Eagle   55
9. Reporters for a Day   64
10. The Invisible Vandal   74
11. A Strange Meeting   81
12. Ghost-to-Ghost Again   90

13. Defeat!   99

14. Jupiter Strikes Back   109

15. Who Is the Smasher?   119

16. A Close Call   126

17. A Smasher Caught!   135

18. The Copycat   143

19. A Thief Unmasked!   150

20. Mr. Sebastian Offers a Challenge   158

A Greeting from Hector Sebastian

Hello again, mystery lovers! And welcome to another extraordinary adventure of The Three Investigators.

In case you haven't met these determined young detectives before, I should tell you that they live in Rocky Beach, California, not far from Hollywood. Jupiter Jones is the leader of the group. Jupe, as his friends call him, has an incredible memory, can repair or rebuild anything, and can practically outthink Einstein. He's also a bit on the . . . stout side. It would be unkind to call him fat, though he *was* once a child actor named Baby Fatso. But that's one fact Jupe would be more than happy to keep a mystery.

Pete Crenshaw, the Second Investigator, is a tall, athletic boy who's a loyal ally in tight spots. But he does get a little nervous when faced with the bizarre or the unexplained.

Last, but by no means least, is Bob Andrews. He's the smallest member of the team, and also the most practical and down-to-earth. Bob's the one who does the research, keeps notes on the Three Investigators' cases, and writes their final reports. I look forward to reading his report at the end of each case.

As for me, I'm Hector Sebastian, former New York private eye and now a mystery writer. I'm one of the boys' biggest fans and am always pleased to introduce their cases.

This case starts with a series of incredible events—car windows shattering all over town for no apparent reason. To find out why, the boys have to patiently dig up facts and make deductions. Along the way they must deal with unknown intruders, electronic wizardry, and suspicious authorities as they come to the aid of a schoolmate who's been falsely accused of vandalism.

So join my clever young friends as they interview the police, track down an invisible troublemaker, and trap a cunning thief. See if you can figure out the solution before Jupiter does. The clues are sprinkled all along the way. Happy hunting!

—Hector Sebastian

1
Broken Windows

"It certainly is a mystery, Mr. Jacobs," the voice of Uncle Titus Jones announced.

Pete Crenshaw raised his head to listen. He was weeding the flower border outside the office cabin in The Jones Salvage Yard one Monday in July. Voices were coming from inside the building.

"Not to me," said an unfamiliar man's voice, presumably Mr. Jacobs'. "Juvenile tomfoolery, that's what it is."

Pete listened eagerly. A mystery!

"Once, even twice, it could simply be an accident," the man went on logically, "but four times? Four times Paul has come home from his friend's house with a truck window smashed. He says he parks and

1

goes inside, and when he comes out to go home the window is broken!"

"That's the truth, Dad," a boy's voice insisted.

"Now come on, Paul." The man laughed humorlessly. "I was a boy once, remember? I expect someone slams the door too hard, or one of your friends clowns around and breaks the window. I'm sure you're protecting a friend, but this is too serious for that."

"Dad! I really don't know how the windows get broken."

"All right, Paul," Mr. Jacobs said calmly. "As I said last Wednesday, until you tell me what really happened, you won't be permitted to drive the truck."

"I've got to pick up and deliver for the store," the boy protested, grasping at a straw.

"You can still load and unload, and help in the store. But I will drive the truck until you find your memory."

If the boy, Paul, said anything in reply, it was too low for Pete to catch. Moments later, Pete heard the front door of the office open. He hurried around the little building and saw a tall man emerge, his face grim and determined. The boy behind him was almost as tall but very thin. He had pale skin, dark hair, a snub nose, and sad brown eyes. The man got into a gray panel truck painted with the legend:

JACOBS' PREVIOUSLY OWNED FURNITURE
ROCKY BEACH, CALIFORNIA
WE BUY AND SELL—FREE DELIVERY

"I'm sorry, Paul," Mr. Jacobs said, "but you must choose between your responsibility to me and your loyalty to your friends. Now get in and I'll take you home. I won't need you anymore today, now that we've delivered the chairs to Mr. Jones."

"I guess I'll walk," Paul said sullenly.

"Suit yourself," Mr. Jacobs replied. He looked down at his son, sighed unhappily, and drove out of the yard. Paul Jacobs stood alone, scuffing his shoe into the dirt and watching the yard helpers, Hans and Konrad, stack the newly delivered chairs.

"Paul!" Pete called from the corner of the office.

The startled boy looked around.

"Over here!"

Paul saw Pete and walked over to him. The two boys knew each other from school, but not well. Paul was several years ahead of Pete and his friends.

"Pete Crenshaw, right?" the snub-nosed boy said.

Pete nodded. "I'm sorry your dad's so mad at you," he sympathized.

Paul sighed glumly. "I just got my driver's license, too."

"Gosh, that's terrible." Pete knew how bad he

would feel if he didn't have a car to drive when he finally got his license. "But maybe we can help you!"

"How?" Paul said unhappily. "And who's *we?*"

Pete pulled a business card out of his shirt pocket. Paul read the card, frowning:

THE THREE INVESTIGATORS
"We Investigate Anything"
?   ?   ?

First Investigator.............. Jupiter Jones
Second Investigator .... Peter Crenshaw
Records and Research .... Bob Andrews

Paul Jacobs nodded, a sudden hope lighting his eyes. "Hey, I remember hearing about you fellows. Maybe you *can* help me."

"Come on!" Pete cried.

The Second Investigator forgot all about his weeding. He dragged Paul Jacobs across the salvage yard to where his fellow junior detectives, Jupiter Jones and Bob Andrews, were nailing up loose boards in the high fence. Jupiter was groaning with the effort of working in the heat. He stopped to rest and wipe his perspiring face after every single blow of the hammer in his pudgy hand. Next to him, Bob grinned as he briskly pounded in nail after nail.

"If there's anything I hate," Jupiter said, "it's a cheerful workman."

"Jupe! Bob!" Pete exclaimed, hurrying up to his friends, Paul Jacobs in tow. "We've got a new case!"

Jupiter's eyes lit up. "Ah-hah, then there's not a moment to lose!" he cried in his best imitation of Sherlock Holmes' English accent. "The game's afoot, fellows!"

He instantly dropped the offending hammer and whirled around, almost bumping into Aunt Mathilda Jones, who had just come up behind him.

"The game may be afoot, you scamp," she said, "but the fence is still awaiting! As for you, Peter Crenshaw, I did not give you weeding tools so you could leave them to melt in the sun. Back to work! None of you rascals has worked an honest hour yet."

"B-but—" Pete stammered. "Paul here has—"

"Another one, eh?" Jupiter's aunt cried. "Good, I have one more job. Your name is Paul, young man?"

"Yes, ma'am," said the bewildered youth.

"Well, Paul, you can—"

At that moment, Uncle Titus came out of the office and headed across the yard. "Lunch!" he cried. "Everyone makes his own sandwich!"

"Food!" Jupiter exclaimed. "That's why we're working so slowly, Aunt Mathilda. We're faint from hunger."

"Starving," Pete groaned, his legs wobbling.

"Weak," Bob whispered. He leaned against an old refrigerator and slid slowly to the ground.

"I only hope I have the strength to reach the house," Jupiter gasped, clutching at the fence for support.

Hands on her hips, Aunt Mathilda sternly watched the performance while Paul Jacobs grinned. She scowled at the staggering boys for a long moment, then burst into laughter.

"Very well, have your lunch. But don't think you've escaped. After you've eaten, it's back to work!"

In the house across the street, the boys made ham-and-cheese sandwiches, then carried them to Jupe's outdoor workshop in the salvage yard. There, between bites of his sandwich, Pete outlined Paul's mystery.

"You have no idea who broke the windows?" Jupiter asked.

Paul shook his head. "I don't even know how they got broken. Once I was out on my friend's porch and even *heard* the window smash, but I didn't see a soul near the truck."

Paul looked at the Three Investigators. "I know it sounds incredible, but the window seems to have smashed all by itself!"

2
The Unseen Force

"It's possible," Jupiter intoned, "for glass to fatigue and shatter spontaneously, but it would be highly unlikely for that to happen four times in close succession on the same vehicle."

Paul Jacobs stared at the First Investigator with glazed eyes.

"What Jupe means," Pete said with a grin, "is that glass can wear out like anything else, but not four times in a row on the same car."

"Thanks," Paul said. "Does he always talk that way?"

"You'll get used to it." Bob laughed. "Underneath, he's just a plain, ordinary genius."

"If you three are finished clowning," the stout leader said frostily, "perhaps we can get on with the case? I suggest Paul tell us everything from the beginning."

"He means"—Pete winked—"take it from the top, Paul."

The snub-nosed teenager smiled, then began his story. It seemed he had a friend who lived at 142 Valerio Street in a residential area of town. Paul often visited his friend's house after dinner, driving there in his father's panel truck. He always parked on the same side of the block in front of the house. Four times in less than two months the window on the driver's side of the truck had been smashed when he came out of his friend's house. Paul had no idea who was responsible for the damage, but he knew it wasn't his pals—no matter what his dad thought.

"Is it always on the same night of the week?" Bob asked.

Paul thought a moment. "I don't think so, but I can't really remember. The most recent time was last Wednesday."

Jupiter looked thoughtful. "Are windows broken in other cars at the same time?"

"Not that I know of," Paul said. "I mean, I've never seen or heard about any other windows being broken on the block—but I never checked."

"Jupe," Pete said slowly, "why is it important about other windows getting broken?"

"If only Paul's windows are broken," Jupiter explained, "then something is wrong with his truck, or someone specifically wants to damage it. But if other windows are broken, then the phenomenon is not limited to one vehicle. Why, Second?"

"Well," Pete said, "my dad had a window on *his* car broken one night last week, and he couldn't figure out how it happened either!"

Pete went on to explain that his father's car had been parked on the street in front of his house, and the window of the driver's seat had been smashed. His father hadn't seen anyone around, and nothing appeared to have fallen through the glass.

"My dad says it was kids. You know, just running around breaking car windows for fun."

"To adults it's always kids." Jupiter sighed, and then his voice became eager. "Pete's information suggests that whatever is going on is a lot bigger than just Paul's panel truck. What we must do—"

Jupiter's round face suddenly went white as a sheet. "Quick, fellows!" he cried. "There's not a moment to lose!"

The other three stared at the stocky leader. Then they all heard it too—Aunt Mathilda's voice booming in the distance: "Time to work, you scamps! I know you're still in the yard. Come out, you scalawags!"

"Paul's too big for Tunnel Two," Jupiter said. "Easy Three, hurry! Run!"

The four boys raced out of the workshop and along the great mound of junk next to it. They stopped at a big oak door still in its frame that was leaning against a pile of large granite blocks. Pete reached deep into a box of junk and brought out a large, rusty key that opened the leaning door. Behind the door was a huge old iron boiler. The four boys stooped to pass through it, and came to a door in the side of a metal structure. Pete opened the door and the boys stepped into a cluttered and cosy room furnished as an office.

"Wow!" Paul stared around in awe. "Where are we, fellows?"

"Inside our Headquarters," Pete explained proudly. "It's an old trailer that Jupe's uncle bought years ago. We piled the junk all around so it's totally hidden, and everyone's forgotten about it. Even Aunt Mathilda's never found us here!"

"It's great," Paul enthused. He looked admiringly at the desk and file cabinet, the telephone with its loudspeaker and answering machine, the radio, intercom, and walkie-talkies.

"It is quite serviceable," Jupiter agreed. "Now, as I was saying when Aunt Mathilda interrupted, what we must do is figure out what could smash a window without being seen and without leaving any traces behind!"

"Ultrasonic waves!" Bob said. "Sound can break glass."

"Sure!" Pete cried. "Like an opera singer."

"Or a jet making a sonic boom when it goes through

the sound barrier," Paul added. "The boom could break glass."

"Do you remember hearing a jet fly over your friend's house just before you heard the window smash?" Jupiter asked Paul.

The older boy shook his head. "No. There was no jet."

"Are there any factories, radio stations, or TV stations near your friend's house?" Jupiter said. "Any machinery that might emit ultrasonic waves by accident?"

"No," Paul said. "There are just houses around."

Pete said, "What about an earthquake?"

"Did you feel anything?" Bob asked Paul.

"No," Paul said, "but maybe there was a real small one. I remember earthquakes I never felt that knocked stuff off shelves."

Jupiter shook his head. "Car windows are very strong."

"How about wind?" Bob suggested. "A tornado? I've read about small local twisters around here."

"Paul would have seen things blowing," Jupiter pointed out.

"M-maybe," Pete stammered, "a ray? A death ray?"

"Like in *Star Wars*," Paul said. "A heat ray or a force ray!"

"From another planet," Bob said.

"A spaceship!"

"An invisible alien!"

"Or . . . a ghost."

"A poltergeist!"

Jupiter held up his hand to quiet the hubbub. "Don't get carried away! There may be an unseen force at work, but most likely there's a simple, obvious explanation that we just haven't thought of. The real problem is that we just don't know enough. I suggest two courses of immediate action to learn all we can about the broken windows."

"What are they, Jupiter?" Paul asked eagerly.

"First, we will duplicate the crime set-up by parking on the street and watching to see if anything smashes our windows. Then—"

"But," Paul interrupted, "my dad won't let me drive the truck anymore."

Jupiter smiled. "I think we can get something much better than your truck for our decoy."

"What's the second action, First?" Bob wanted to know.

"We'll use a Ghost-to-Ghost Hookup!"

Paul gasped. "A ghost to what?"

"A Ghost-to-Ghost Hookup," Pete explained. "It's a way Jupiter invented to get a whole lot of kids all looking or watching for something. Each of us calls five friends and asks them to do whatever it is we want, and then they call five of their friends, et cetera."

"I get it," Paul said. "If each of us has five friends, and each of them has five, and all those have five . . . Wow, that would be five hundred kids! We could cover Los Angeles with a plan like that."

"Exactly," Jupiter said. "But let's limit our coverage to Rocky Beach. We'll use the hookup to find out if any other car windows in town have been smashed over the last two months, and just when and where."

"Which should we do first?" Pete wondered.

"We can do them both at the same time," Jupiter said. "We'll set up the Ghost-to-Ghost, and our answering machine can collect the reports as the kids phone in. Meanwhile, we can all go out and try to attract the crime!"

"Trap whoever's smashing the car windows," Bob said.

"Or *what*ever is doing it," Jupiter said. "After all, it *could* be some unseen force no one's ever heard of!"

3
The Scene of the Crime

It was almost dark as Pete biked rapidly toward the salvage yard. The extra piece of pecan pie that had made him late lay heavy in his stomach. As he neared the yard he saw a magnificent sight in front of the main gates. It was the gold-plated Rolls-Royce that the boys often used on their cases. Paul Jacobs stood nearby, staring in amazement at the great black-and-gold automobile.

"What in the world is *that?*" he demanded as Pete rode up.

"It's an antique Rolls-Royce," Pete replied matter-of-factly, and explained how Jupiter had won thirty days' use of it in a contest when the boys had first formed the Three Investigators team. Later a grateful client had arranged for the boys to have the use

14

of the car any time they wanted, together with its chauffeur from the rental agency, the Englishman Worthington. Just as Pete finished his story, Jupiter and Bob hurried out through the main gate.

"You're both late," Jupiter said. "Records and I had to set up the whole Ghost-to-Ghost ourselves."

"My dad made me walk," Paul explained. "I'm sorry, fellows."

"And you, Second?" Jupiter's eyes twinkled. "An extra piece of pie, I expect."

Pete gaped. "How did you know?"

"Pure logic," Jupiter said airily. "Clear reasoning."

Bob laughed. "We called your house. Your mother told us about the pie. Jupe's just jealous."

"Only small minds are jealous," Jupiter said loftily. "Anyway, Mrs. Crenshaw said she would save me a piece of the pie."

As they laughed, the front door of the Rolls-Royce opened and a powerfully built man with a lean, good-humored face stepped out. He wore a chauffeur's uniform, complete with cap, which he now held in his hands.

"Good evening, Master Jones," he said gravely.

"Good evening, Worthington," Jupiter replied. "We will have a guest with us on tonight's mission: Paul Jacobs."

Worthington bowed to the older boy. "Master Jacobs."

"We're in a hurry tonight, Worthington," Jupiter said. "We must reach 142 Valerio Street by precisely nine o'clock."

"That should present no difficulty," the chauffeur said. "If you will all enter the vehicle now."

As soon as they were on their way, Jupiter rapidly outlined his plan. They would drive to the corner of Valerio Street, where he, Bob, and Pete would slip out. Worthington and Paul would drive on around the corner and park where Paul always did. Paul would get out of the Rolls and loudly announce that Worthington could take some time off because he was going to be in his friend's house over an hour. Worthington would then walk off as if going for coffee, while Paul would go up to his friend's house. But instead of going in, Paul would hide where he could watch the Rolls-Royce from the sidewalk side. By then the Three Investigators would have sneaked up and hidden on the other side of the street.

"I'm afraid there could be some minor damage to the Rolls-Royce, Worthington," Jupiter added uneasily.

"Are we on a case, Master Jones?"

"Yes, we are."

"Then it will be in the line of duty," the chauffeur responded quietly. "What, may I ask, might the nature of the damage be?"

"Possibly a broken window."

Worthington sighed. "Very well, sir."

"Or," Jupiter added, "perhaps a dent or two."

Worthington's eyes traveled lovingly over the gleaming black-and-gold hood of the car, and he seemed to shudder.

"Well," Jupiter said hastily, "maybe only a side window."

"A window, sir, and I shall be content."

By then they had reached the corner of Valerio Street. Worthington brought the car to a silent stop, and Jupe's plan went into effect. A few minutes later the Rolls was parked in front of 142 Valerio and the Three Investigators were settled behind a clump of bushes directly across the street from it. There was plenty of cover on the block, thanks to the many trees and bushes in the deep front yards. They made the street seem closed in and secretive.

The Investigators watched as Paul Jacobs and Worthington spoke their rehearsed dialogue. Finally Paul went up the concrete walk to his friend's large stucco house and disappeared into the shadows of its front porch. Worthington walked away down the block, whistling a jaunty British march, and then the street became silent. The Investigators waited in the dark.

It was Pete who saw the woman first.

"Look, fellows," he whispered.

A tall woman wearing slacks and a man's shirt was walking a Great Dane in the warm summer night.

She walked not on the sidewalk but out in the street, and she carried a shiny black cane with a heavy silver head. The gigantic dog pulled her along as it sniffed at every curbside tree and automobile tire along the way. Suddenly, the woman stopped. She had seen the dazzling Rolls-Royce. She stood looking at the car in admiration until the Great Dane lunged toward it and almost pulled her over.

The woman raised the silver-headed black cane directly in front of the driver's window of the great car. She swung the cane wildly.

"Stay, Hamlet!" she commanded.

The dog cowered, its tongue lolling out, every muscle quivering. The woman went on waving the heavy cane, coming perilously close to the Rolls-Royce's window.

"That's a dumb way to train a dog," Pete whispered. "She'll just make it afraid of her."

"Could she have broken the windows with that cane?" Bob wondered. "I mean, by accident?"

Jupiter shook his head. "Paul would have seen her."

The woman finally lowered the menacing cane, and the dog happily dragged her off along the street. They had barely turned the far corner when two boys in Little League uniforms came from the same direction, playing catch with a baseball. One was in the street and one on the sidewalk. They threw the ball over the parked cars and ran to make clowning catches in the dark. Half the time they missed the ball and had to chase it among the cars.

Bob whispered, "Jupe? Could they have done it?"

"No," the stout leader whispered back. "Even at night Paul couldn't have missed them."

"Anyway," Pete muttered, "those two couldn't hit anything even by accident."

They watched the two boys play their way down the dark block and onto the next street. The block became quiet again. It was growing late. The windows in most of the houses were dark now. An hour passed with no movement along the empty street. Then a tall man on a ten-speed bicycle rode around the far corner.

The hidden boys came alert. The single light of the bike probed ahead like the antenna of some insect. The rider was dressed in a colorful yellow cycling shirt and shiny black cycling tights that ended just below his knees. He wore high yellow socks and narrow shoes held to the pedals by toe clips. With his backpack, helmet, goggles, and earphone attached to a radio or cassette player in the backpack, he looked like an alien from another planet.

"He's right out of *Star Trek*." Pete giggled softly.

The cyclist rode slowly along the block. When he saw the Rolls-Royce he almost came to a stop, then began to ride in circles beside the gleaming black-and-gold car. The boys held their breath in anticipation as the cyclist circled and stared at the antique automobile. But seconds later he suddenly straightened his bike and rode away into the deeper darkness of the next block.

"Gee," Pete whispered, "for a minute I thought—"

"He looked like he'd do something," Bob groaned.

Jupiter frowned in the dark behind the bushes. "We're too eager, jumping at shadows. We must be patient."

The boys stretched their cramped muscles and went on waiting. Jupiter shifted nervously. Soon Paul would be leaving his friend's house.

A quick movement caught Jupe's eyes. Someone was walking among the shadows at the far corner. Behind trees. Near the parked cars. Flitting back and forth between the street and the trees and lawns.

A small man moving furtively, carrying something.

"What's he got?" Pete hissed, staring.

The little man continued to skulk along the block from trees to cars, looking all around him as if afraid of the shadows themselves. Then he flitted out into the street, carrying something long and thick.

"It's a baseball bat!" Bob exclaimed, almost too loud.

Transfixed, the boys watched the man slip among the cars toward the gleaming Rolls-Royce. They could all imagine him swinging the heavy bat against the windows of the great car. Imagine the shattering glass.

Imagine that up on the porch of 142, Paul would hear the glass smash but fail to see the furtive little man slipping away along the street. They waited for all this to happen—but the man only hurried on as if someone were chasing him. He disappeared from the block without having swung the baseball bat at anything.

Pete groaned in disappointment.

Equally dejected, the other boys said nothing more for some time as they silently watched the dark, deserted street. No one walked along. No cars drove past. Eleven o'clock came with no further incident.

"Paul always went home by eleven," Pete said.

Jupiter stood up. "If we are to duplicate the conditions properly, we too must leave now."

He stepped out into the dark street just as Paul Jacobs emerged from the shadows of his friend's porch and Worthington appeared from the far end of the block. As they all gathered beside the Rolls-Royce, Jupiter looked at the others glumly.

"Perhaps," the stocky leader said, "I was wrong."

"Wrong, Jupe?" Bob asked. "How?"

"I assumed that because Pete's dad had a window broken too, the smasher wasn't just after Paul's panel truck," the First Investigator explained. "But Mr. Crenshaw's window could have been a coincidence. Maybe the Jacobs' truck *was* the only real target."

"If that's true, then reenacting the crime with the

Rolls-Royce wouldn't work," Pete realized. "We'd have to use the panel truck."

"Jupe?" Bob said slowly. "In that case the Ghost-to-Ghost Hookup wouldn't work either. There won't be any other smashed windows."

"That's right, Records," Jupiter agreed dismally. "Well, it's too late to return to Headquarters tonight. We'll have to wait until morning to find out if the Ghost-to-Ghost did any good at all!"

4
Alarm!

Wondering about this strange new mystery, Bob tossed restlessly all night and overslept. He was rushing downstairs when he heard his father's angry voice.

"It's not safe on the streets anymore!"

"I'm sure it was an accident, dear," Mrs. Andrews' voice answered. "Many things can smash a car window by accident."

"Well, the car goes into the garage from now on."

Bob almost fell down the last few stairs and into the kitchen, where his parents were finishing breakfast.

"Dad! Was your car window smashed last night?"

"I'm afraid so, son."

"The driver's seat window?"

"Yes," Mr. Andrews said, frowning up at Bob. "How did you—?"

"And you don't know how it got broken?" Bob burst out excitedly. "You didn't find anything that could have smashed it?"

"How do you know so much?" Mr. Andrews asked, sounding suspicious.

Bob told his father about Paul's mystery, Mr. Crenshaw's broken car window, and the boys' vigil the night before.

"And you're sure this Paul Jacobs saw nothing at all when he heard his truck window break?" Mr. Andrews asked.

"Not a thing, Dad."

"But it has to be vandals!"

"Then they're invisible vandals, Dad. Ghosts."

"That's ridiculous, Robert! You know—"

"I'm sure there's some simple explanation," Mrs. Andrews broke in. "Jupiter and the boys will solve it. Now finish your breakfast, both of you."

Bob wolfed his eggs, anxious to get to the salvage yard and tell the others that at least one car window had been smashed last night. He finished with a gulp of milk and jumped up.

"Is your bed made, young man?" Mrs. Andrews said.

"Yes, Mom!"

He biked as fast as he could to the yard. But instead

of going in through the main gate, he rode along the
front fence. Artists of Rocky Beach had painted the
boards with trees, flowers, lakes, swans, and even a
shipwreck scene. Bob stopped at the shipwreck,
pushed against the eye of a painted fish that was
peering at the sinking vessel, and two green boards
swung up. This was Green Gate One, which opened
into Jupe's workshop. No one was in the workshop,
but Pete's bike was there. Bob quickly crawled through
Tunnel Two—a length of wide pipe which led under
a mass of junk to the Investigators' Headquarters—
and pushed up through the trap door in the trailer's
floor.

"Hey, guys! Last night my dad's—"

Bob stopped and stared. No one was listening to
him. In fact no one was even aware that he'd arrived.
The office was as frantic and bustling as NASA on a
launch day. Jupiter, Pete, and Paul Jacobs were all
standing before a giant map of Rocky Beach pinned
on a wall, sticking pushpins into the map as a re-
corded voice droned in the background:

"*. . . Mr. Wallace had his driver's seat window
broken in front of 27 East Cota last Wednesday.*"

Paul stuck a pushpin into the map, and a different
voice announced, "*Joe Eller found his car window
smashed a couple of weeks ago near 45 West Oak.
Front left window.*" Pete pushed a pin into the map.
Then a girl's voice filled the room: "*Mrs. Janowski*

of 1689 De La Vina found her driver's seat window broken last Monday night." Jupiter stuck a pin in the map.

Bob tapped Jupiter on the shoulder. "The Ghost-to-Ghost is working!" he exclaimed.

Jupe turned and grinned triumphantly. "The answering machine is full of reports from last night and early this morning, and calls are still coming in over the phone. Car windows have been broken all over Rocky Beach for the last two months!"

"It always happens to the driver's window, always on a car parked on the street," Pete cried, "and no one's ever seen who—or what—did it!"

"We've got almost a hundred pins in the map," Paul said.

"A hundred and one," Bob said, and told them about his dad's car.

"Put it on the map," Pete said.

Bob took a handful of the pushpins, stuck one into the map at his own house, then joined the others in listening to the Ghost-to-Ghost messages. Soon the reports on the answering machine ended, but the telephone continued to ring with more news of broken windows. Jupe taped the new calls for the record while the others listened to them over the loud-speaker:

". . . *next to the driver's seat on the car of Mr. Andrews on—*"

Bob said, "That's Max Brownmiller on the next block. I guess he heard about my father's car."

The boys continued to listen and stick pins in the map until the phone finally stopped ringing. Pete counted the pins in the map.

"One hundred and twenty-seven!"

"The first was two months ago." Paul said. "Even before my window was smashed the first time."

"So Jupe was right," Bob said. "The window smasher isn't just after Mr. Jacobs or Paul."

"But," Jupiter said slowly, staring at the map with its silver pushpins on almost every street in the middle of town, "what's the pattern? The M.O.?"

"M.O.?" Paul said, puzzled.

"Method of Operation," Bob explained. "When something happens over and over you can usually find at least one thing about it that keeps repeating. Like maybe the windows are always broken on the same kind of car because someone has a grudge against a certain auto maker."

"Or," Pete said, "maybe somebody hates beach people for making too much noise, so all the pins would be around the beach."

"Or if the windows were broken by some natural force," Jupiter added, "then all the pins would be near the source. But the pins are everywhere."

"Not everywhere, Jupiter," Paul pointed out. "Only in the center of town. We don't have any pins out this way around the salvage yard, or down by the beach, or up in the mountains."

The others nodded.

Bob frowned. "Jupe?" he said. "There *is* something kind of peculiar."

"What's that, Records?"

"Well," Bob said, staring at the map, "windows were reported smashed all along Valerio Street last night, so why weren't any windows broken on the block where we were?"

Jupiter nodded. "I noticed that, but I can't think of an explanation right now. There must be a reason, and I'm convinced it's hidden in those pins on the map. I think we should listen again to the answering machine, and—"

A sudden metallic clang seemed to vibrate through the entire trailer. It sounded as if something hard had struck some metal object in the mound of junk surrounding Headquarters. It came again, along with a faint clattering noise.

"Someone's out there!" Pete exclaimed.

The sounds came again.

"Maybe it's Aunt Mathilda or Uncle Titus, Jupe," Bob said. "I'll take a look out through the See-All."

He hurried to a corner of the room where an ordinary length of stovepipe ran up through the roof of the trailer. The bottom of the pipe ended in an elbow and had two smaller pipes attached for handles. It looked very much like the viewing end of a periscope, and that's exactly what it was—a homemade periscope of pipe and mirrors which Jupiter had built so that the Investigators could see out from inside the trailer. Bob peered into the eyepiece, turning the viewer all around.

"I see Aunt Mathilda and Uncle Titus over at the main gate," he reported. "Hans and Konrad are loading the truck. A few customers are poking around on the far side of the yard. No one's near here."

The metallic sounds rang out once more, closer this time, as if someone were sneaking across the mound of junk around the trailer.

"It must be some intruder!" Pete declared.

"He's below my field of view!" wailed Bob.

"Quick, fellows," Jupiter urged. "Bob, you go out Tunnel Two. Pete can use Door Four. I'll take Easy Three. We'll try to surround whoever it is. You stay in here, Paul. Don't open any of the doors unless you hear the secret code: three knocks, then one, then two."

Paul nodded as the three junior detectives slipped out in search of the mysterious intruder.

5
Menace in the Junkyard

At the end of Tunnel Two, Bob peered out cautiously.

A slim figure, all in black, was crouched at the far corner of the outdoor workshop!

The intruder seemed to be working at something on the ground. Bob strained to see what it was. His shoulder struck the side of the pipe, dislodging some junk outside with a loud clatter.

The black figure whirled. It had no face!

Then Bob saw the reflection of two sharp eyes, and realized that the rest of the head and face was covered by a black ski hood. The eyes were staring straight at Bob. He'd been spotted!

"Who are you? What do you want?" Bob shouted as he crawled out of the pipe.

The dark shape grabbed whatever it had been working on and darted out of the workshop into the yard. Bob leaped up and ran to the workshop entrance. He saw the fleeing shape threading like a deer among the stacks of junk straight toward Easy Three! Jupiter would catch him!

The intruder disappeared from view behind a pile of old bricks. Bob listened, but a minute passed and he heard nothing. Where was Jupiter?

After another couple of minutes Bob trotted quietly to the spot where he had last seen the black figure. But no one was near the brick pile. He lay down flat and crawled to the corner of a stack of lumber and peered around that. A sudden movement caught his eye. Someone was sneaking along the side fence.

Bob watched, holding his breath. Whoever it was had no hood covering his face. A shaft of sunlight fell across the figure. It was Pete! Bob jumped up. Pete saw him and waved silently, using arm and hand signals to let him know he hadn't seen or heard anything. Bob made a thumbs-up sign to indicate he had seen the intruder.

Just then a loud clatter of wood falling came from directly ahead!

Bob waved violently to Pete, signaling that they should circle around and meet at the spot where the clatter had come from. Pete nodded and vanished. Bob began to work his way carefully among piles of discarded furniture collected by Uncle Titus. He finally reached the stack of lumber that had collapsed or been knocked over in front of a large heap of junk, one almost as large as the mound that hid Headquarters. Pete appeared at the other side of the heap.

"Did you see him?" Bob mouthed.

"No one." Pete shook his head.

"Help!"

Both boys froze. The cry had come from somewhere inside the large mound.

"Help!"

Pete said, "It's Jupe!"

"Hurry," Bob urged.

They plunged in among the rows of densely packed junk, twisting their way through the narrow passages.

"Help!"

The muffled call seemed to come from their left.

"Help!"

Now it came from the right.

Bob and Pete stood deep inside the towering mass of salvage and looked all around. It was impossible to move in a straight path. Frantically, they wove their way through the maze of narrow corridors, blocked by sudden dead ends, piles of old doors that had fallen over, jumbles of concrete blocks and ancient appliances.

"Help!"

"Jupe!" Pete called. "If you can hear us, keep yelling!"

"So we can tell where you are!" Bob shouted.

"*Help . . . Help . . . Help . . . Help . . . !*"

The cries of the First Investigator guided them along the twisted lanes of junk, now sounding nearer, now farther, until suddenly the cries seemed to be somewhere very close to them.

"There!" Bob exclaimed.

It was an old butcher's walk-in freezer. A two-by-four had been braced under the heavy latch so that the door could not be opened from inside. The muffled cries had stopped.

"Quick! There's not much air in there!" Pete cried.

They knocked the two-by-four aside and swung open the heavy door.

"Jupe?" Bob cried.

The First Investigator sat slumped against the rear wall of the bare freezer, meat hooks and racks all around him. He didn't move.

"First?" Pete said anxiously. "Are you okay?"

The stocky leader sighed. "The old open-door trick," he said, disgusted. "And I fell for it like a complete amateur."

"Who was it, Jupe?" Bob asked. "Did you see?"

"All I saw was a shadow in black when I came out of Easy Three. He saw me and ran this way after knocking over that lumber. I chased after, but I only got occasional glimpses of him among all these stacks. Then I saw him run into this freezer. At least I thought I did. He must have just ducked behind the opened door, because when I got here and looked inside, he was *behind* me. He pushed me in and slammed the door. I pushed the inside latch to get out, but the door wouldn't open."

"You could have run out of air!" Bob exclaimed.

Jupiter sighed again. "This old freezer is so full of holes there was actually no danger of that, Records. He fooled me, fellows, and I have no idea who he was or what he looks like."

Thwangggg! Crash!

Another loud clatter echoed through the salvage yard. This time it sounded like something metallic was falling. The three boys hurried out of the old freezer.

"He's still in the yard!" Pete cried.

"Maybe he had as hard a time getting out of here as we had getting in!" Bob said.

"Come on, fellows," Jupiter urged.

The Investigators threaded their way back out as fast as they could. Once they reached the more open space of the yard, they hurried in the direction of the last crash. It had come from somewhere near the back fence. The boys ran all the way to the fence without glimpsing the shadowy figure or hearing any more noises.

"Look!" Pete cried. "Up there."

A six-foot overhang of tin ran along the entire fence to protect the better junk from sun and rain. Hooked over the lip of the overhang was what looked like a small four-pronged anchor, with a thick cord knotted to a ring at the top of its shank.

"What is it?" Bob wondered.

"A grappling hook, or climbing hook," Jupiter said. "You throw it up and catch it on a wall or fence or cliff so you can climb up on the rope!"

As the Investigators stood staring up at the big hook, the rope attached to it suddenly rolled up in a moving loop like a snake. The hook flipped off the edge of the overhang and was dragged clattering back across the tin to fall outside the yard.

"Quick!" Jupiter cried. "Red Gate Rover!"

As the boys ran along the fence to their secret rear exit, they heard the roar of a car engine in the street outside. Bob hurriedly released a catch on the fence, three boards swung up, and the boys scrambled through to the street just in time to see a small red car vanish around a corner.

"Too late," Pete groaned.

"Did anyone see what it was? Get the license?" Bob cried.

"It could have been an MG," Pete declared, then added, "but I'm not sure, and I didn't see the license plate."

"Neither did I," Jupiter admitted.

They stood in the now deserted street and looked after the vanished car.

"What was he doing here?" Bob wondered.

"He sure wanted to get into the yard without being seen," Pete said. "Bringing that hook and rope."

"Let's go get Paul," Jupiter decided, "then see if we can figure out what our unknown intruder was up to."

The Investigators hurried back to their secret gate. On it a small painted dog sadly regarded a burning building in a large mural of the 1906 San Francisco Fire. One of the dog's eyes was formed by a knot in the wood. Jupiter picked it out, reached in, and released the catch that let the three boards of Red Gate Rover swing up. Once inside, the boys used Door Four, following a narrow corridor through junk until they reached a sliding panel at the rear of their hidden trailer. Jupiter knocked: three, one, two.

"What happened?" Paul asked eagerly as he opened the panel.

Jupiter told him, then asked, "Does the intruder sound like anyone you know, Paul?"

"No," Paul said. "What was he doing out there?"

"That is what we must discover," Jupiter declared. "Let's go out and search through the junk around the trailer. Maybe we can find some clue that will tell us what the intruder was up to."

Jupiter led the way out to his workshop. "From the sounds we heard," he said, "our visitor must have been climbing on the mound itself, so one of us should search up there."

"Bob's the lightest, I guess," Paul said.

"Boy, he sure is!" Pete laughed.

"I am aware of Records' weight, Second," Jupiter said huffily. "Bob will climb the mound. The rest of us will—"

"Ah-hah!" The voice boomed out like doom. "Caught you, you young scamps!"

Aunt Mathilda stood at the workshop entrance, hands on her hips. There was no way the boys could escape without diving into Tunnel Two and revealing their secret hideout.

"Peter Crenshaw, you left the weeding half-done yesterday. And Jupiter Jones, there are still loose boards in the fence. You and Bob get to nailing. Your new friend can help Peter."

"B-but . . . we're on an important case," Jupiter stammered.

"Fiddlesticks! No work, no visitors to the yard all summer! I mean what I say, young man."

She turned on her heel and stalked off. The four boys glumly watched her disappear toward the yard office.

"There goes our case," Pete groaned.

"She can make it awful hard for us to meet," Bob agreed.

Jupiter nodded. "We'll have to finish our jobs, yes. But no one said we can't combine Aunt Mathilda's work with our own. So two of us will work on the weeding and fence-mending, while the other two get back to the business of searching for clues. We can switch jobs every hour or so."

Everyone agreed. By midafternoon they had made good progress on the fence and flower border and had even managed to eat some lunch. But they had found little evidence of the intruder.

"He was up on the mound, all right," Bob reported. "Some of the junk that hides our telephone line's been kicked away. I put it back, but it sure was moved."

It was late afternoon when Paul discovered a tiny silver-colored disc less than half the size and thickness of a dime.

"It was in the workshop near your intercom," Paul explained. "I wouldn't have seen it at all except it flashed in the sun."

The Investigators crowded around.

"It's a battery for miniature electronic devices,"

Jupiter exclaimed. "Was there anything else where you found it? Any small microphones or transmitters?"

"Just this," said Paul, holding out his hand. In it were some small shards of plastic and tiny scraps of wire.

"Looks like somebody stepped on it, whatever it was," said Bob.

Jupe studied the pieces and then announced, "I think it was a bug."

"You mean somebody was spying on us? Listening to what we said?" cried Pete.

"Exactly," said Jupe. "Everybody look for another bug—a little plastic box, or something that looks like a miniature microphone, or anything electronic."

But by dinnertime the boys had found nothing more. Aunt Mathilda surveyed their work and warned Jupiter he had better finish the next day. Gloomily, the boys gathered in the workshop.

"The Ghost-to-Ghost," Jupiter said, "has proven that car windows are being broken all over town—too many of them to be a coincidence. There must be some reason for the smashing. We must learn *why* it's being done before we can discover *who* it's being done by."

"But how, Jupiter?" Paul wondered.

"We must study the pins in the map. I'm convinced the answer is there somewhere. Also, we will reenact the crime again. I'm sure the Rolls-Royce will lure the smasher sooner or later."

"Tonight, Jupe?" Bob asked eagerly.

"No, it's too late to get the car tonight. We'll try again tomorrow night. Perhaps this time the smasher will strike and we can catch him in the act!"

6
Jupiter Finds an M.O.

Paul had to work in his father's shop the next day. With no investigating to be done until evening, Bob and Pete went surfing and then had dinner at the Crenshaws'. No one heard from Jupiter all day.

It was eight thirty, and Jupiter still hadn't called, when Bob and Pete rode into the salvage yard. There was no sign of anyone in the workshop. The boys crawled into Tunnel Two and reached the trap door up into Headquarters. There was no sound inside the hidden trailer, but narrow lines of light showed around the door. The boys sensed someone was up there.

Slowly, Bob pushed up the trap door. The two boys poked their heads warily into the lighted room.

Jupiter sat in a chair, his eyes wide and bright but

glazed as if he had been looking at the same thing for too long.

"I think I have the answer, fellows," he said as they climbed up into the room. He was staring straight ahead, not looking at them. "But I don't know what it is!"

"You know"—Pete blinked—"but you don't—"

"The pushpins!" Bob broke in, following Jupiter's gaze across the room to the map of Rocky Beach. The pushpins were still in it, but they were no longer silver-colored.

"Wow," Pete said, "all different colors!"

"Four different colors, to be exact, Second," Jupiter corrected him. "I've been here all afternoon, staring at the map and trying to find a pattern. I decided to use different-colored pins for each day of the week. It was soon obvious that only two colors were needed—one for Mondays and one for Wednesdays. All the windows have been broken on Mondays and Wednesdays only!"

"But," Bob said, "there are four colors of pins, not two."

"Yes." Jupiter nodded. "With only two colors, I still couldn't see any pattern or method of operation. So I decided to try a different color for each *different* Monday and Wednesday of the last two weeks: yellow, red, green, and blue." He paused dramatically. "And an M.O. appeared immediately!"

Bob was staring at the map. "They're all in straight rows. Each different color goes across the map in a straight line!"

"Quite correct, Records," Jupiter acknowledged. "Every Monday and Wednesday for the last two weeks, and probably for six weeks before that, car windows have been smashed in a straight line across Rocky Beach."

"Wow!" Pete exclaimed. "Does that mean . . . ? Is that . . . ? Gee, what *does* it mean, Jupe?"

"Well," Jupiter admitted, "I'm not actually sure yet."

Bob and Pete looked at Jupiter, then at the map with its colorful pins, and then back at Jupiter again.

The First Investigator sighed. "As I said, fellows, I think I have the answer, but I don't know what it means. I do see one more important fact on the map."

"What, Jupe?" Bob demanded.

"On each night that the windows were smashed, at least two blocks on the street were missed! No windows broken."

Pete stared at the map. "You mean each time the window smasher goes along a street he skips a couple of blocks?"

"That's correct." Jupiter nodded. "Look at the line of yellow pins along Valerio Street, where we were on Monday night. Three blocks were missed, and one was the block we were watching!"

"Gosh, Jupe, why?" Pete frowned.

"I can't answer that yet either," Jupiter said, "but since it's part of an earlier pattern, it apparently had nothing to do with our surveillance. There must be another reason why our block was missed that night, and other blocks were missed other nights."

Bob studied the map. "The missed blocks don't seem to have anything in common, Jupe. I mean, they're not in any special part of town, or even near each other. They're not even the same blocks in each row—like, say, the fifth and sixth block every time."

"But they do have *something* in common," Jupiter said. "They are always consecutive. They always come one after the other."

Bob and Pete looked at the map and nodded. The empty spaces in the rows of colored pins were always together. As the three boys considered the possible significance of this, a soft knocking came at the door of Easy Three—three, one, two. Bob opened the side door, and Paul Jacobs came hurrying in.

"Sorry I'm late, fellows. I tried to tell my dad what the Ghost-to-Ghost had proved to us, but he wouldn't even listen."

"Adults," Jupiter said, "can be awfully obtuse."

"Yeah," Paul said doubtfully. "Anyway, Worthington and the Rolls-Royce are at the front gate."

"Then," Jupiter declared, "we must begin tonight's mission!"

7
Accused!

As the big Rolls-Royce moved silently through the Rocky Beach night, Worthington spoke over his shoulder.

"A strange thing happened at the rental agency yesterday morning, Master Jones. Someone telephoned to say he was eager to contact four boys he had observed riding in our gold-plated Rolls-Royce. He called himself Mr. Toyota and explained that he needed four typical American boys to pose for advertising photographs, one of whom, you will forgive me, Master Jones, must be quite stout. Thinking to help, our clerk gave them your address at the salvage yard."

In the dark back seat the four boys looked quickly at each other.

"It must have been that intruder tracing us!" Bob said.

Jupiter asked, "Can you describe the voice, Worthington?"

"Our clerk said it was muffled, as if from a poor connection, but had a definite high, Oriental inflection. However, I suspect our clerk is not an authority on accents."

"Sounds like a disguised voice to me," Bob said.

"I agree, Records." Jupiter nodded.

"But," Paul said, "it means someone did see us Monday night! Maybe that's why nothing happened."

Jupiter thought a moment. "No, he apparently saw us *in* the Rolls. That would have been before or after we were hidden. If it was before, we hadn't even reached Valerio Street yet, and he couldn't have known where we were going. If after, then it would have been too late to change what happened. Besides, the smasher was skipping blocks before we even knew about the case."

"You're right," Paul agreed. "It couldn't mean anything."

"On the contrary," Jupiter declared. "It could mean something vital. If the intruder has some connection with the smashed windows, then someone is very worried about our investigation!"

Worthington said softly, "Valerio Street coming up next, gentlemen."

The boys quickly repeated their actions of the previous Monday, and soon Pete, Bob, and Jupiter were hidden behind the same bushes across the street from number 142. They settled down to watch as Paul went up the walk to his friend's house and Worthington strode away down the block.

Soon the tall woman with the Great Dane came along, still carrying her silver-headed cane. Once again she stopped to admire the Rolls-Royce, and again she waved the cane as the leaping dog tried to pull her along.

"Stay, Hamlet!"

Behind the bushes the boys stifled their giggles as the woman was dragged around the corner by her gangly pet. The street became silent again. None of the occasional passing cars even slowed down, much less stopped. Then the man on the ten-speed bike rode out of the darkness with his headlight piercing the night. This time he didn't even pause to admire the gleaming Rolls. Like some weird spaceman in his helmet and goggles, he rode straight into the next block and disappeared.

Behind the bushes the boys waited.

It was after ten when a gaudy Volkswagen turned the corner and drove slowly along Valerio Street. Painted purple and yellow, its fenders battered and its bumpers falling off, it rumbled down the street toward the Rolls-Royce. As it passed, something flew out of its window and vanished under the Rolls!

"They threw something under the Rolls!" Pete exclaimed.

"What was it?" Jupiter cried.

Abandoning their cover, the Investigators ran across the street to the Rolls. Peering under the car, they saw a brown paper bag with something inside it. Pete fell on his stomach and pulled out the bag.

"Hurry, Second!" Jupiter urged.

Pete stood up and tore open the bag. A puzzled look passed over his face when he saw what it contained.

"A beer can," he said, disgusted. "They just threw out an empty beer can!"

He flung the can away over his shoulder.

"Second!" Jupiter cried.

In his frustration, Pete had unthinkingly hurled the can behind him—straight at the Rolls-Royce! It struck the rear window of the gleaming car, bounced off, and clattered along the street.

"Wow," Pete breathed in relief, "I'm sure glad it—"

Suddenly the quiet night was filled with sound. Whistles began to blow. Voices shouted all along the dim street! Uniformed policemen ran out from behind the trees and bushes in the yard of the house on the right, leaped from behind the hedge of the house to the left. Red and white lights revolving on top, sirens wailing, police cars screeched around both corners!

Men and cars all converged on the three boys, who stood frozen beside the Rolls-Royce. In an instant they were securely in police hands and surrounded by an angry crowd. A grim-faced sergeant strode up.

"So, got you vandals at last!"

As the three boys stood speechless with shock, a furious voice began shouting from behind the circle of police.

"You young scoundrels! Thieves! Villains!"

The circle of police parted and a wild-eyed old man waving a cane limped angrily toward the Investigators. Wearing an old black suit badly in need of pressing, a black string tie, and a gold watch chain across his vest, he pulled away from his companions—a young man and a girl in her late teens—who seemed to be trying to restrain him. Brandishing his cane, the old man advanced on the boys.

"Thieves! Where is my eagle?"

A small, dapper police lieutenant whose gold collar bar looked brand-new climbed out of one of the patrol cars with flashing lights.

"All right, you three, you want to tell us why you've been smashing car windows?" the lieutenant said, eyeing them severely. "Just for fun, or is there something more behind it? Eh?"

"Make them tell you where my eagle is!" the old man raged.

Pete gulped, then stammered, "W-we didn't break any windows! We're working to find—"

"Don't try to lie, kid," the sergeant said.

Bob cried, "But Officer, we're here to catch the window smasher ourselves! We're detectives."

"You are making a grave mistake, Sergeant," Jupiter said angrily. "If you will look at our credentials, everything will be quickly explained."

Jupiter reached toward his pocket. All the policemen came to attention, touching their pistols.

The dapper little lieutenant pointed sharply at Jupiter and said, "Hold it right there! Keep your hands out of your pockets!"

Jupiter froze. As all the policemen watched him, there was another commotion on the outskirts of the circle. A patrolman came through the crowd dragging Paul Jacobs.

"Got another one, Lieutenant. Came right up and said he was a friend of these three."

The cane-waving old man cried, "I know him! He's been here every time they broke the panel truck windows!"

"It's my dad's truck!" Paul protested. "I was driving it."

The little lieutenant smiled. "And I suppose this is your dad's Rolls-Royce too, kid."

"Search them!" the old man demanded. "One of them might be carrying the eagle!"

Jupiter drew himself up to his most haughty height and gave the wispy-haired old man a withering stare. "We have broken nothing, sir, and we have stolen nothing."

"Especially not a big bird like an eagle," Pete exclaimed.

"He must be crazy!" Bob cried. "How could we carry an eagle around!"

"The man," Jupiter said, "is clearly demented."

The sergeant glared at the boys. "Don't try to be so clever. We're on to you. We caught you red-handed, attempting to break the Rolls-Royce window with that can."

"It was an accident," Pete insisted. "I just threw it away."

"If we wanted to break a car window, we'd use something heavier than an empty beer can," Bob pointed out. "It's too light."

"A bag was thrown out of a purple-and-yellow Volkswagen that drove past a couple of minutes ago," Jupiter explained. "It went under the Rolls-Royce, and Pete here pulled it out to see what was in it. When he found it was only an empty beer can, he threw it away in disgust and simply failed to look where he was throwing it, Sergeant."

"Liars!" the wild old man cried.

Before anyone realized what was happening, he raised his cane and hit Jupiter over the head!

Thwock!

Stunned, Jupiter stood helplessly. Everyone was paralyzed for a moment. Pete, Bob, and Paul were still being held in check by the policemen, and the young man and teenage girl were too far behind the old man to stop him. He raised his cane again.

Through the circle of police Worthington suddenly appeared and with a single movement caught the cane in midair, tore it from the old man's grasp, and flung it away.

"You will refrain from striking Master Jones, my good man!"

The old man blinked at Worthington, then turned to the police.

"My cane!" he shrieked. "He attacked me! You saw him! He's the ringleader!"

As the distraught old man tried to punch the chauffeur, Worthington placed one hand on his assailant's head and calmly held him off while addressing the police.

"May I inquire why you are detaining my young employers," the elegant chauffeur asked, "and what mental institution this unfortunate old gentleman escaped from?"

The sergeant and lieutenant stared at the imperturbable chauffeur, who maintained his composure while restraining the disheveled old man with one hand.

"You're the driver of this Rolls-Royce?" the lieutenant said suspiciously.

"I am," Worthington acknowledged.

"And you say you work for these kids?" the sergeant said. "They own the Rolls-Royce?"

The outraged old man was still trying to reach Worthington with his futile flailing. "More likely they work for him! Kids wouldn't know the value of the eagle! He's the thief! Arrest him!"

Worthington frowned and glanced toward the two young people behind the old man.

"If you two are related to this gentleman, I suggest you remove him. I fear he may hurt himself."

The young man and the girl hurried to grab the violent old man and pull him away. Worthington brushed his hands fastidiously as he turned back to the police.

"No, Officer, the Three Investigators do not own the Rolls-Royce, but they are renting it from my agency and therefore are my present employers. If you wish to verify these facts, you may call my permanent employer, the Rent-'n-Ride Auto Rental Company."

"The Three Investigators?" the sergeant repeated, incredulous.

"That," Jupiter said haughtily, "is the name of our

junior detective firm. As I have tried to inform you,
we are investigating the case of the smashed windows. That is why—"

"Don't listen to that fat thief!" the old man cried
as he struggled to break away from his young companions.

"I can confirm Master Jones' statement, Officer,"
Worthington said, "and vouch completely for the three
boys."

"They can't really be detectives, can they?" the
young man asked. "I mean, they're just kids."

"We saw them throw that can at the Rolls-Royce,"
the girl said.

The lieutenant and sergeant looked from one to
the other of the boys and then at each other. The
lieutenant sighed wearily.

"I wish someone could tell us what's really going
on!"

A new voice spoke from the street behind them.
"I think I can do that, Lieutenant."

8
A Stolen Eagle

Chief Reynolds of the Rocky Beach police walked through the crowd of onlookers toward the lieutenant and sergeant. He nodded to the Three Investigators and Worthington, then spoke to the suddenly nervous lieutenant.

"At least I can tell you, Samuels, that everything I've heard the boys and Worthington tell you is absolutely true. They are The Three Investigators detective team; they often rent the Rolls-Royce; they certainly wouldn't smash windows or steal anything; and if they say they are working on the case—why, then they are."

"Yessir," Lieutenant Samuels said.

"Since you never met the boys, you couldn't be expected to know all that," the chief said. "But if you had looked at their credentials, you would have seen a card from me vouching for them."

"We did see that taller boy throw a can at the Rolls-Royce, Chief," the sergeant said defensively. "It's been almost two months since we started the stake-outs, and it really looked as if we'd finally caught the vandals."

"I admit it's been a frustrating case," Chief Reynolds conceded before turning to the Investigators. "How did you happen to get into all this, boys?" he asked.

Jupiter told him about Paul Jacobs and the panel truck, and Mr. Jacobs' suspicion that his son knew more about the smashed windows than he was admitting.

"I'm afraid adults do tend to suspect young people when vandalism is involved," the chief said, and looked toward the dapper Lieutenant Samuels. "Even the police."

"How long have the police been on the case, sir?" Jupiter asked. "Why were your men staked out on this particular block?"

"We've been on the case for almost six weeks now, Jupiter," the chief explained. "Ever since it became clear that the smashed windows were not isolated incidents. For some reason, car windows are being broken all over town. My men have been watching in various locations. They've been on this block for three nights."

"Have they seen anything, Chief?" Bob asked.

"Not a thing, Bob. Absolutely nothing suspicious—until tonight, that is." The chief grinned. "The windows go on being smashed all over town, but never on the blocks where my men are watching."

"Hmm," Jupiter mused. "That's been our experience too, although this is only our second stakeout."

"Chief?" Bob said, "what was all that about a stolen eagle?"

Chief Reynolds looked at the old man in the black suit, who stood glaring at the boys and the police. His wispy gray hair was still disheveled, but someone had returned his cane. He was brandishing it again as he observed the scene and made angry comments to his young helpers.

"Last week," the chief explained, "Mr. Jarvis Temple there reported that the eagle had been stolen from his locked car in front of his house—it's the next house up, behind all the trees. He had inadvertently left the eagle in the car. Later that night he realized what he'd done, and went out to get the eagle. But he found that the passenger-seat window was smashed and the eagle was gone."

"If the window was broken," Bob said, "maybe the eagle just flew away."

"No, Records," Pete said, "it would have been in a cage. Eagles are very dangerous. But I sure don't understand how anybody could forget an eagle!"

Old Jarvis Temple was still glowering suspiciously at the boys. Now he pulled away from his companions and limped forward, once more wielding the cane.

"Liars! Thieves! Pretending they don't know what we're talking about. Bird indeed! They know—"

Jupiter's eyes suddenly gleamed. "Of course! You don't mean a real eagle—you mean a coin! A rare coin!"

"A very rare coin." Chief Reynolds nodded.

"American," Jupiter remembered. "A gold coin with a face value of ten dollars and minted in the early eighteen hundreds, I believe. It has an eagle pictured on it, so that's why it's called an eagle. The half eagle, or five-dollar gold piece, of 1822 is one of the rarest coins in the world."

"You hear!" Jarvis Temple roared. "The scoundrel knows all about coins!"

"Jupiter knows all about everything," Pete said with a grin.

"Well, almost everything." Chief Reynolds smiled. "But I assure you, Mr. Temple, the boy is not a thief."

Jarvis Temple huffed and glared at Jupiter. The

young man with him touched his shoulder as if to soothe him, and smiled at the Investigators and Chief Reynolds.

"My uncle is just upset, Chief. Of course we believe you. I'm glad to meet such bright boys. I'm Willard Temple, boys, and this is my cousin Sarah."

The girl with him nodded.

"Just how much is your eagle worth?" Jupiter asked.

"Actually," Willard Temple said, "ours is a double eagle."

"A twenty-dollar gold piece," Jupiter explained. "The rarest is the one of 1849. There's only one, and it's owned by the government. They once refused a million dollars for it!"

"Yes," Willard Temple said, "and there are only three of the 1853 over 2 in existence, each worth half a million."

"What over what?" Pete blinked.

"A coin dated 1852 with a 3 stamped over the 2 to make it an 1853 coin," Jupiter explained.

"Right," Willard Temple said. "Ours is the ultra high relief double eagle of 1907. There are only a few of them known to be in existence. Ours is uncirculated, and there isn't a scratch on it. It's worth at least two hundred and fifty thousand dollars."

"Why was it in the car at all?" Bob wondered.

"We were bringing it back from an exhibition,"

Sarah Temple said. "Uncle just left it on his seat when he got out."

She was a tall, slim girl of eighteen or nineteen, dressed in an army shirt and blue jeans and wearing oversized tinted glasses even now at night. She smiled at the boys, especially Paul. Her uncle glared at her as angrily as he had at the boys and the police. Crankiness seemed to be part of his personality.

"My niece drives too fast and keeps that CB radio of hers on all the time. I become so nervous it exhausts me. It would exhaust anyone in his right mind! I had to get out of that car and rest, and I simply forgot the box. I left it on the passenger seat. When I went back to get it, I saw the smashed window even before I reached the car. My eagle was gone!"

As if overcome by the tragedy of his loss, Jarvis Temple sat down on the curb and held his head in his hands. His nephew bent down to comfort him. Willard Temple was a short, lean young man in his twenties, with lighter hair than his brunette cousin Sarah. His business suit was almost as conservative as his uncle's.

"Collectors become most attached to their coins," Jupiter observed sympathetically.

"Gosh," Pete said, "you think maybe all the windows got broken to steal something from the cars?"

Jupiter shook his head. "There couldn't be that

many valuables left in cars on the street, Second."

"Besides," Paul Jacobs said, "nothing was stolen from our panel truck."

"Or my dad's car," Bob added.

Willard Temple stood up again. "But what other reason could there be for breaking car windows?"

"It has to be some organized gang of thieves," Sarah Temple said.

Chief Reynolds shook his head. "No, the boys are right. There hasn't been a single stolen property report from any of the other car owners involved. Most of the damaged cars weren't even locked. It's far more probable that we're dealing with just plain vandalism."

"I don't know, Chief," Bob objected. "Wouldn't you have caught ordinary vandals by now? Or at least scared them off?"

"Simple vandalism doesn't usually have an organized M.O., does it, Chief Reynolds?" Jupiter asked thoughtfully, and filled the chief in on the conclusions they'd drawn from their map and colored pushpins.

"Mondays and Wednesdays and always in a straight line?" the chief said, frowning. "That does sound like an organized M.O. But why? All that organization doesn't make sense if someone just wants to smash some car windows. There must be more to it."

"It is puzzling, sir," Jupiter acknowledged. "Still,

I'm convinced that some simple answer does exist. Can we continue to work on the case, Chief?"

"I don't suppose I could stop you anyway," Chief Reynolds said with a smile, "but be careful, boys. Remember, there's a thief out there with a coin worth a quarter of a million dollars. If you find any evidence relating to the eagle you're to call me immediately. You'll do nothing on your own. Is that clear, boys?"

Chief Reynolds looked at each of the boys in turn, and then at Worthington. They all nodded solemnly.

"Of course, Chief," Jupiter said. "But would it be possible for us to see the reports of all your stake-outs?"

"I'm sorry, Jupiter, but that's confidential department business."

Jupiter chewed on his lower lip, crestfallen.

"Chief," Bob said, "would it be okay for a reporter from my dad's newspaper to talk to some of the policemen who worked on the stakeouts? I mean, ask some questions about what happened?"

The chief's eyes twinkled. "Well, I don't see why not, Bob. Freedom of the press, eh? Of course, the reporters would need proper credentials."

"Oh, we'll—" Bob paused and grinned. "I mean, *they'll* have full credentials, sir."

Chief Reynolds laughed, and then his face grew serious. "Actually, boys, my men and I have been over those reports many times without finding anything significant. I'm afraid you'll just be wasting your time."

"Perhaps so, sir," Jupiter said. "But we'd like to try. You never know what some new eyes will find."

The chief nodded soberly, but under his uniform cap his eyes twinkled again.

9
Reporters for a Day

It was barely eight o'clock when the four boys gathered at Bob's house the next morning. The Records and Research man had told his father what was needed, and Mr. Andrews had come through with the proper press credentials.

"I'm officially hiring all of you as stringers, or freelance reporters, for one dollar a day, and assigning you to interview various policemen concerning their search for the car-window smasher."

Mr. Andrews handed each boy a check for one dollar and an official press card. "Now you work for my newspaper, if only for today."

"Thanks, Dad," Bob said. "We really appreciate it. A lot."

The other young sleuths added a chorus of thanks, went out to their bikes, and headed straight downtown to police headquarters. Paul Jacobs rode a rusty old bike he'd dug out of his garage.

"Each of us will go in alone and ask to interview a policeman who took part in the stakeouts. Show your credentials, and if there's any objection tell them Chief Reynolds said it would be okay. That way we'll get four different men," Jupiter explained as they rode along.

"What do we ask them, Jupe?" Pete wanted to know.

"We want to hear about anything unusual they might have seen, anything special that happened," Jupiter said, "but above all, we want to know everyone who passed them each night as far as they can remember."

Pete went into police headquarters first, and then Bob. By the time Jupiter followed Paul in and approached the duty sergeant, it took all his powers of persuasion, plus a none-too-subtle suggestion that the sergeant might want to call Chief Reynolds, before the First Investigator was finally allowed to question a policeman.

Pete met the young patrolman in his squad car just as the man was about to go out on his shift.

"Those stakeouts on the window smashings? Not a

thing, kid. No one suspicious at all, you know? A real waste of time. We should all have been out stopping real crimes, not hiding to catch a bunch of kids."

"You're sure that it's only kids smashing the windows?" Pete asked.

"It's got to be, Crenshaw," the young policeman said. "And I'm not going to be a patrolman forever, you can bet on that. So a stakeout for some rotten kids who smash car windows isn't my idea of important police work like I should be doing, you know?"

"Well, what about people going by? Did you see a lot of them?"

"Oh, we saw plenty of people going by," the patrolman said. "That's all we did see—people going by, and going by, and going by! No one ever stopped. No one threw anything at the car windows or whacked them with a hammer or anything."

"Just who *did* you see going by?" Pete asked. "Can you remember?"

"Of course I remember. I remember them all. I'm going to be a detective pretty soon, so you bet I remember. Everyone important anyway."

"I'll write them down," Pete said, opening his notebook.

The young policeman looked at the notebook and cleared his throat nervously. "Well, let's see. The first night I was on the watch there were, er, well an old guy in a Cadillac who parked and hung around awhile before a lady came out of a house and they drove off. And . . . er, yeah, two old ladies walking dogs and two guys on bikes. One of the guys had a helmet and goggles and was listening to something in his backpack through an earphone. Earphones're dangerous, you know? A lot of states have laws against using earphones and headphones when driving a car or riding motorcycles or bikes."

"Who else did you see?" Pete persisted.

"Huh? Well, I don't know. Just a lot of people doing nothing. I mean, we knew it was kids, so why watch so hard, okay?"

The sergeant who met Bob in one of the interrogation rooms offered him a Coke and smiled. He had met the Investigators before.

"So, now you're a reporter, Bob? I thought you boys were detectives."

"We are, Sergeant Trevino, but we have to find out what you all saw on your stakeouts. The chief says we can't read the reports."

"No, you'd need a court order," Sergeant Trevino agreed. "Does the chief know you've become reporters?"

"It was his idea, in a way. Freedom of the press and all."

The policeman laughed. "Okay, ask your questions then."

"We know you didn't see any windows broken, sir, but did you see anything else suspicious?"

"Not even faintly suspicious," the sergeant said. "Everyone who stopped on those nights lived on the block and did nothing except park and go into their houses."

"Then, what about all the people and vehicles that passed by without doing anything? Do you remember any of them?"

"Of course I do. I wrote it all down," Sergeant Trevino said, pulling a small notebook out of his shirt pocket and riffling through it. "There were two men in a green Cadillac who just drove by; a man with a beard in a gray Volkswagen; a boy on a bike delivering the newspaper; two elderly ladies with a boy carrying a slingshot; four people walking their dogs; a—"

"Did one of them have a silver-headed cane and a Great Dane?" Bob asked quickly. "The dog-walkers, I mean."

Sergeant Trevino consulted his notebook. "No, there were two poodles—a standard and a miniature—one Schnauzer, and a Doberman."

"Oh," Bob said, disappointed.

The sergeant went on reading from his notebook: "Two boys in Little League uniforms playing catch; a long-haired young man in a Porsche; a man wearing a helmet, goggles, backpack, and an earphone and riding a bike; three members of a motorcycle gang called the Gray Death; two Chevrolet station wagons that seemed to be following each other; four joggers in sweatsuits; three men who were apparently late getting home from work; a special-delivery mailman; three boys in Boy Scout uniforms who came back about two hours later; two hobos . . ."

Paul interviewed his policeman in the locker room where the man was changing into civilian clothes after his duty shift. He was a short patrolman who kept looking at his watch.

"I'm ready to ride out, kid. Nothing happened on those stakeouts anyway."

"I'll be as fast as I can, sir," Paul said.

The patrolman frowned. "Okay, what do you want to know?"

"Well, we know you didn't see any windows broken, but did you notice anything suspicious or maybe just unusual?"

"Nope, not a thing." He looked again at his watch, pulled on his second motorcycle boot, and stood up, ready to leave.

Paul hurried on. "Can you tell me who you saw those nights?" he stammered. "I mean, everyone who passed the stakeouts?"

"Everyone?" The patrolman stared at Paul.

"Uh, yessir, if you can remember."

"You got to be kidding, kid! Everyone who walked

by and didn't do anything at all?" He yawned. "Look, I made my report. Nothing happened. Now I've got things to do, okay?" he said, heading toward the door.

"I'm sorry. I guess it's hard to remember that far back."

The short patrolman stopped and turned back. "What do you mean? You think I don't remember the stake-outs? At least anything worth remembering, not just people who didn't do anything? I sure remember all the false alarms."

"False alarms?" Paul said quickly.

The short policeman nodded. "We had some real beauts."

"Tell me about them," Paul said.

The weary officer looked at his watch once more and sighed. "Okay. There was this old pickup truck. It had a gang of kids in the back singing and raising all kinds of ruckus. Halfway up the block we were watching, the whole gang stopped and piled out of the truck. For a while we were sure they were going to start smashing windows. But in the end they just played a wild game of follow-the-leader over fences and fire hydrants and bushes and even the cars until they reached the corner. Then they piled back into the pickup and drove off."

Paul wrote it all down. The tired patrolman yawned again before continuing.

"Then there were three motorcycle-gang punks: the Gray Death gang. They cruised the block real slow and started circling in figure eights, looking in all the car windows as if they wanted to steal something, only they never actually stopped their bikes. They finally went on to the next block, still circling."

Paul made some more notes and nodded. The young policeman sighed again.

"Last, there was this tall guy all decked out like some space nut with earphones and riding a ten-speed. For a minute it looked like he was going to pull something out from under his biking shirt as he slowed down, but then he just speeded up and rode away down the block."

Paul went on writing and nodding for a time after the policeman had finished. When he looked up, he was all alone. The tired patrolman had gone home.

The dapper Lieutenant Samuels stared straight at Jupiter.

"I don't believe in kids who think they're smart enough to solve crimes, Jones. All they do is get in the way of the real police."

"I'm sorry you feel that way, sir," Jupiter said politely. "However, Chief Reynolds does not, apparently, agree with you. We have been able to render him valuable assistance on some occasions."

Lieutenant Samuels flushed. "You really think you kids are as good as trained policemen?"

"Perhaps not, sir. But sometimes we can do things the police can't do—precisely because we *are* kids."

Samuels glared at the stout young sleuth, then sat down in his small office. He did not offer Jupiter a seat.

"What do you want from me?"

"Just a description of everyone who passed your stakeouts at any time."

"Is that all?" the lieutenant said sarcastically. "You know no one could recall all of that, and the written record is part of the official report, which the chief already told you was confidential."

"He said the actual report was confidential," Jupiter pointed out. "But he said we could ask you about anything you put into it, and I'm sure you keep good notes, Lieutenant."

Obviously trapped, the lieutenant swiveled in his desk chair. Then his angry eyes brightened. "All right, but I go on duty in five minutes. You can come back when I'm finished in about eight hours; or I'll have one of our clerks type up the information from my notes when she has time, and you can just wait outside."

Jupiter had no choice but to wait in the corridor. Even Chief Reynolds would agree that the lieutenant's work came first. He waited on a bench for over three hours, with Samuels passing every now and then and smiling nastily. The other boys were finished and long gone by the time Jupiter finally got the typed notes. He read them quickly, stood up, and hurried out to his bike.

10
The Invisible Vandal

"The man on the ten-speed!" Pete cried.

"Wearing the helmet, goggles, backpack, and ear-phone!" Paul echoed.

"All three of our interviewees saw him pass their stakeouts," Bob said, "and he passed us both times too!"

The chorus greeted Jupiter as he pushed up the trap door and emerged from Tunnel Two into Headquarters. The stocky leader of the team sat down and stared again at the large map with the straight lines of colored pins across it.

"He was seen by Lieutenant Samuels too," Jupiter put in, "but neither we nor the lieutenant saw him actually *do* anything. Did any of your policemen see him breaking a window? Or even doing something suspicious?"

"Well," Paul replied, "the patrolman I talked to said it looked for a while as if the man on the bike was going to take something out from under his biking shirt."

"And he stopped and rode around staring at the Rolls-Royce the first night we watched," Bob added.

"But he never actually did anything," Jupiter said. "It could be that he simply rides home from somewhere every night and takes different streets for variety."

"You mean it's just a coincidence?" Pete said, sounding disappointed.

"On the other hand," Jupiter went on, his eyes brightening, "he *is* the only person who's appeared at *all* the stakeouts we know about. And, since windows are never broken on blocks where the police are, the fact that he hasn't been seen breaking a window doesn't rule him out."

"You think the smasher knows where the police are watching, Jupe?" Bob asked.

"It would appear that way, Records." Jupiter nodded.

"But no windows got broken when we watched either," Pete said.

"The police were on our block too, Second," Jupiter pointed out.

"You mean he didn't know about us, but he knew the cops were there?"

"Exactly," Jupiter said. "The man on the bicycle is our prime suspect at the moment. All we have to do now is prove he's guilty."

"Great," Pete said. "How do we do that?"

"You have something in mind, First?" Bob asked.

Before Jupiter could answer, Paul, who had been looking more and more confused, broke in.

"But," the older boy said, "if the man on the bicycle is breaking the windows, how is he doing it? Why didn't I see him? I mean, if he doesn't stop and whack the windows with something, how does he break them? And if he does stop, why didn't I see him the night I heard the window smash?"

Bob looked at Jupiter. "How *do* you break a window from a moving bicycle, First?"

"Or stop and smash a window without being seen?" Pete asked. "Unless you can make yourself invisible." The Second Investigator gulped. "Forget I said that, fellows."

"I think we can rule out invisibility, Second. Except perhaps psychological invisibility," Jupiter said, and turned to Paul. "When you heard your truck window break, you saw no one near the truck. But perhaps you saw something passing on the street. Something already past when you heard the smash. Maybe just a glimpse of something moving on toward the corner. Something you saw yet didn't *really* see."

Paul frowned, half closing his eyes as if to envision that dim night more clearly in his mind. "I didn't see anyone around the truck, like I said. And I'm sure there wasn't anything out on the street. I mean, I didn't see . . ." The older boy's voice trailed off and his frown slowly deepened. "Wait! Maybe something *did* . . . sort of move. Out on the street *ahead* of the truck. Just . . . moving, you know? Not a car or anything, just . . . someone?"

"Like a kind of *impression* you can't quite remember?" Jupiter prompted.

"I did see something." Paul nodded, trying to remember, trying to recall the dark street that night. "But . . . I forgot I saw anything as soon as it was gone."

Jupiter nodded. "We all have a tendency not to notice things or people or actions so familiar, so common, we see them almost every day. So common that after a while we see them but we don't *know* we've seen them. We forget them as soon as they're gone. The mailman, the garbage men, the meter reader, delivery boys, door-to-door salesmen, and a man just riding a bike down the street at night. Especially if we're distracted by the sound of a window being smashed. We see the biker without really paying much attention to him, and then the window smashes. We don't connect a man on a bike with a broken car window; the window claims all our attention, and we forget we ever saw the biker at all. Psychological invisibility."

"But that would mean he didn't stop to smash the window, First," Bob said. "So how does he break windows from a moving bike?"

"And how does he always happen to miss the block the police are on?" Pete wondered.

"We don't know enough to answer those questions yet," Jupiter said, "but I have some ideas. I want to talk to Chief Reynolds again, and I want to examine Paul's panel truck."

"Sure," Paul said. "We can do that anytime. It's at our shop right now—my dad's out of town."

"But, Jupe," Bob objected, "you still haven't told us how we're going to prove the man on the ten-speed is smashing the windows—if he is."

"We're going to catch him in the act, Records," Jupiter declared, "by using the Ghost-to-Ghost Hookup again."

"You mean tell all the kids on the Hookup to watch for him and see what he does?" Pete said.

"That's just what I mean," Jupiter said grimly. "This time we know exactly what we want them to watch for. If the man on the bike is the window smasher, the Hookup shouldn't have much trouble proving it."

"Unless he knows they're all watching, the way he knows the police are," Pete said. "I mean, maybe he's got X-ray vision. Or infra-red eyes that see in the dark! Maybe he's psychic, or has ESP and can feel when people are watching him!"

"I suspect, Second, that the way our smasher knows the police's whereabouts involves something much simpler," Jupiter said. "In any event, we can't put our plan into effect until next Monday. The smasher won't strike again until then."

"That's lucky for me," Pete declared. "I've got to go away with my folks this weekend."

"And I have to mind the shop while my dad's out of town," Paul said, "so I'll be busy all weekend."

"Then I suggest we go and examine your panel truck now," Jupiter said.

They were halfway out Easy Three when the telephone shrilled. Startled, they looked at one another. Except when the Ghost-to-Ghost Hookup was operating, hardly anyone ever called them at Headquarters. Jupiter activated the phone's loudspeaker.

"The Three Investigators," he announced in his most imposing voice.

"Er," said a nervous voice that sounded familiar, "may I speak to Mr. Jupiter Jones?"

"Jupiter Jones speaking," the rotund leader replied.

"Ah, Jupiter. This is Willard Temple. We met the other night in front of my uncle Jarvis's house."

"I remember, Mr. Temple. How can I help you?"

"Well, my uncle has been thinking over what Chief Reynolds said about you boys, and he's wondering if perhaps he should hire you to help find the eagle. He asked me to call and discuss your charges."

"We don't charge, Mr. Temple. We just try to help people solve problems, and if they want to give us something to help our work, that would be fine."

"I see. Well, that sounds quite fair. Er, my uncle still isn't sure. Perhaps you could come over here now and we could discuss it some more?"

"Now?" Jupiter said. "Well, all right."

"You know our house? Number 140 Valerio?"

"We'll be right over, Mr. Temple," Jupiter said. The other three boys nodded eagerly.

11
A Strange Meeting

Number 140 Valerio was next door to Paul's friend's house. It was the one to the right, almost hidden by trees and bushes, where the police had been staked out the night before. The boys left their bikes in the driveway at the side, where a four-door Buick sedan waited sedately. In the garage at the rear they could see an ancient Cadillac that looked as if it hadn't moved in years. Canvas covered the hood and windshield.

A gravel path led up to the house among the trees and bushes. With so much greenery, the street was almost invisible from the front door. Jupiter rang the bell, and the four boys stood waiting expectantly. Nothing happened.

"You're sure he said to come right away?" Pete asked.

"That's what he said," Jupiter replied.

Suddenly from somewhere in the house they heard voices—angry voices a long way off. Jupiter rang again repeatedly. There was still no answer, but now the voices had stopped.

"Maybe this bell doesn't work," Bob said.

"There could be a side door they use," Pete suggested.

The boys returned to the driveway and looked for a side or back door. They found nothing on the garage side of the house.

"What's that?" Paul said, staring.

In the open backyard a four-foot-wide metal saucer on three spindly legs stood aimed up at the sky.

"It's a satellite dish," Jupiter said.

"It receives signals from satellites in space," Bob explained. "TV and radio signals are bounced off a satellite so we can get programs live from New York or Europe or even China. With one of these dishes you can get the programs without paying a cable company."

"That sure sounds like Jarvis Temple," Pete said.

"*Boys?*"

The call came from the front of the house. The boys hurried around to the front door again. Willard

Temple was on the steps, looking around in confusion.

"Ah, there you are."

"No one answered," Jupiter said, "so we went to look for another door."

"I was in the back of the house getting instructions from my uncle. Come in."

The short, slender nephew of old Jarvis Temple led them along a wide Victorian entry hall shining with a polished parquet floor, and through sliding doors into a large, formal living room with ugly old-fashioned furniture. Willard Temple was again dressed in a conservative dark suit. He smiled stiffly at the boys.

"My uncle isn't feeling very strong today, boys, so he's decided to rest. He asked me to discuss the possibility of your working for him to secure the return of the eagle."

"Actually," Bob said, "we're already on the case. We're working with Paul to catch the window smasher, and that's the same thing."

"Of course," Willard Temple said. "I'd forgotten that."

"Still," Jupiter put in quickly, "I don't see any reason we can't try to find your eagle as well. It might help us catch the smasher if we knew where the coin could be sold and who would buy it."

"Gosh," Pete said, "wouldn't it be real hard to sell? I mean, everyone knows all about it, right? Everyone would know it was stolen. So who'd want to buy it?"

"Collectors can be unscrupulous, Second," Jupiter said. "Most wouldn't touch the coin, of course, but there are some who would want it under any circumstances. Just to own it, to look at in private—never even letting anyone know they had it."

Willard Temple nodded. "He's right, boys. There are few such collectors, but some of them are among the wealthiest and could pay almost any price. As for where the coin might be sold, there are always some disreputable dealers to accommodate such collectors."

"Still," Jupiter said, "it would be difficult. The thief would have to know how to contact an unscrupulous dealer or collector."

"Very difficult," Willard Temple agreed. "He'd have to be quite familiar with the entire world of coin collecting."

"Perhaps you could tell us who some of these illegal dealers are," Jupiter said, "so we could watch them."

"Me?" Young Temple shook his head, running his fingers nervously through his light brown hair. "No, I'm afraid I can't tell you much about the coin world. I've never been able to get very interested in my uncle's hobby."

"Then we'll have to ask him," Jupiter said.

Willard Temple blinked. "My uncle? Oh, of course. As soon as he feels up to it, if he decides to hire you." He looked at his wristwatch. "Well . . ."

Jupiter was glancing around the old-fashioned living room. "Perhaps we could examine some of your uncle's other coins? So we know what we're looking for? I don't see any coins in here."

"Oh, no, we keep them in his study," Willard Temple said, and glanced at his watch again.

"Could we see the coins?" Jupiter pressed.

"See? Yes, of course. This way."

He led them out of the living room and along the center hallway to a door at the rear. He opened the door with a key on his ring. The small study was all dark wood and books, with a heavy maroon rug on the floor and rows of glass display cases on legs. In the cases were coins of every description, all nestled in dark blue velvet. Willard Temple pointed to one cabinet.

"Those are the American coins. That one at the top left is Uncle Jarvis's only other double eagle. It's not worth nearly as much."

The boys crowded around the case to examine the large gold coin in its blue velvet niche. It glistened under the light inside the cabinet. About the size of a silver dollar, the coin showed a flying eagle in profile, wings raised above its head, against the expanding rays of a rising sun.

"How old is it?" asked Bob.

"This one is from 1909," said Willard Temple. "The date is on the other side with a standing figure of Liberty. It's a beautiful coin, but only worth about eighteen thousand dollars."

Pete whistled. "Sounds like a pretty good price to me. And the coin isn't even very old."

"It's not the date that's important. It's the rarity and the condition. Not many gold coins were minted early in this century because paper money became more popular than heavy coins."

"But why is your stolen eagle worth so very much more?" Paul asked. "A quarter of a million dollars is incredible!"

"Ah, the stolen coin is in ultra high relief. That means the Eagle and Liberty stand up much higher from the background. It's the same design—both are by Augustus Saint-Gaudens—but the ultra high relief version was only minted in one year, 1907. It's extremely beautiful and extremely rare."

"What kind of box was the stolen eagle in?" Bob asked.

"A black leather jeweler's case the size of a cigarette package, with two hinges and a button-released catch," Willard Temple explained. "Inside it has the same blue velvet as the display case. But the coin was in a clear plastic envelope to protect it from wear."

Bob, Pete, and Paul stared at the magnificent gold

coin as they listened to Willard Temple. Jupiter looked around the room.

"Sir?" the stout leader said. "I haven't seen any TV sets in your house."

"My uncle hates television." Willard Temple laughed. "He won't have a set in the house."

"Then why is there a satellite dish in your back-yard?"

"Dish?" The nephew blinked again. "Oh, Sarah and I have a TV set in the game room. My uncle's resting in there now, or I could show you what the satellite dish does."

"I see," Jupiter said, nodding. "Then I suppose we must return later, or can you hire us for your uncle?"

"I think—" Willard Temple began.

Suddenly, the door of the study was flung open, and old Jarvis Temple himself stood in the doorway, leaning on his cane and staring at the boys.

"What are they doing in my study!" the old man roared, limping into the room. "Trying to decide what coin to steal next?"

"Your nephew let us in, sir," Jupiter said quietly. "If we are to help find your eagle, we need to know what it looks like. Now, if you could tell us—"

"Help find my eagle!" The rumpled, gray-haired man stared in astonishment. "I wouldn't let you four within a mile of my eagle! Get out of my house!"

"But your nephew—" Jupiter began.

Pete broke in hotly, "He called us and said you wanted to talk about hiring us! We wouldn't—"

Old Jarvis turned purple. "My nephew is a liar! Hire you? I'll have none of that! Get out, I say!"

He raised his cane menacingly and lunged at the four boys. But before the cane could descend on any of them, Sarah Temple rushed into the room and tore it out of the furious old man's hand.

"Uncle! What are you doing!"

The tall girl stood with the cane, looking at her uncle in horror. Jarvis glared at her.

"I don't know what you two think you're doing, but I want those juvenile delinquents out of my house right now!"

With that, the old man grabbed his cane back and limped out of the study. Willard and Sarah watched him go in dismay. The dark-haired girl, an inch taller than her older cousin, still wore her oversized sunglasses, but was dressed in a red leotard and tights as if she had been exercising. She looked sadly after her uncle.

"We're sorry, boys. My uncle has spells of forgetfulness these days. It's the strain of the loss of the double eagle. I heard him ask Willard to call you, but he just doesn't remember. I guess, though, we'd better not hire you officially until he's more rational."

Willard Temple nodded. "I'll call you again if he changes his mind."

Outside the big Victorian house, the boys walked down the driveway to their bikes.

"Gee," Paul said, "old Jarvis completely forgot he told Willard to call us."

"I wonder," Pete mused. "The old man sounded pretty alert to me."

"Yes," Jupiter agreed thoughtfully, gazing at the small red Datsun now parked in the driveway. "Anyway, we'd better go see what we can find in Paul's panel truck before it gets dark."

12
Ghost-to-Ghost Again

The gray panel truck was parked in the alley behind Mr. Jacobs' used-furniture shop. The four boys searched the seat, the floor space in front of the seat, and the interior of the truck.

"I guess a paper clip wouldn't break any windows," Pete said as he held up the bent clip he had found under the seat.

"Hardly, Second," Jupiter said dryly.

"Or some empty soda cans?" Bob added from the back of the truck where he had found a bunch of empty cans.

"I get thirsty working," Paul confessed with a laugh. "Then I forget the empties. My dad gets mad at that too."

"What's this?" Pete asked. He held up a small,

misshapen piece of grayish metal about the size of a thumbtack.

Bob took it. "Looks like one of those little round sinkers you put on a fishing line for kelp bass."

"One that got stepped on and mashed," Paul said, studying it.

"A split-shot sinker," Jupiter said, peering at the lump of metal. "But this isn't lead, and it looks as if it was hollow before it got mashed. At least, part of it was."

"Maybe it was the top to some kind of little pouring can," Pete suggested. "You know, oil or glue or something like that."

Bob held up the small blob. "See those little ridges on one side? There's something familiar about them, but I can't put my finger on it."

"Well," Pete said, "it sure isn't large enough to smash a window. But I think I'll hang on to it anyway. It might be part of something else."

Pete took the little hunk of metal and dropped it into his pocket, and the boys continued their search of the truck. There were rubber bands and pennies and crumpled credit card receipts for gasoline and all the varied debris that gathers on a vehicle's floor. But there was nothing large enough to have been thrown through a rolled-up window. The boys gave the truck another quick once-over and then gave up.

The afternoon was ending as the Investigators said

goodbye to Paul and rode their bikes back to the salvage yard. Aunt Mathilda was standing outside the office cabin.

"A man named Willard Temple called, Jupiter. He said to tell you that his uncle had definitely changed his mind and he's sorry he bothered you. Whatever that means."

"Gee," Pete lamented, "I thought we had a real paying client."

"At least a reward if we found his coin," Bob agreed.

"Aunt Mathilda?" Jupiter said slowly. "Did you see anyone acting strange outside the yard today? Perhaps climbing on a telephone pole?"

"Acting strange? Not a soul," Aunt Mathilda replied.

"Well, maybe not strange," Jupiter said. "But did anybody climb that pole back there?"

He pointed to the telephone pole that held all the wires leading into the salvage yard.

"No." His aunt shook her head. "Except the telephone man, of course."

"When was that, Aunt Mathilda?" Jupiter asked quickly.

"Why, this afternoon. I think it was before you boys left, but I'm really not sure. Who notices a telephone man?"

When the Investigators had moved out of Aunt Mathilda's hearing, Pete turned to Jupiter.

"What's all this about a telephone man, First?"

"You think maybe the telephone man wasn't really a telephone man?" Bob said. "Maybe someone trying to peek inside the yard?"

"Possibly, Records," Jupiter answered. "However, that will have to wait. Since there's nothing more we can do until Monday night, I suggest you two spend the weekend thinking of our basic problem: Is the man on the bicycle smashing the windows? And if he is, how is he doing it and why? Also, how does he always seem to know where the police are watching?"

"Is that all you're going to do, Jupe?" Bob asked.

"Aside from a visit to Chief Reynolds, yes, Records. With Pete out of town and Paul busy working, there won't be much else we can do."

By the time Monday came, the four boys were all itching for action. They met early at Headquarters and spent the day setting up the second Ghost-to-Ghost Hookup. They gave all their friends an exact description of the tall man on the ten-speed, telling them to pass it on to *their* friends, and so on, and asking everyone to watch for him. All the watchers were instructed to remain inside their houses if possible, or at least to watch from a well-concealed hiding place. Jupe then connected the answering machine to record all reports, and activated its speaker. Everything was in readiness for the evening's activities.

It was already growing dark when the four boys gathered after dinner in Headquarters. They sat around the answering machine and waited. Eight o'clock came and went. The boys fidgeted and spoke to each other in whispers, as if someone might hear them . . . as if they too were on watch with the widespread network of "ghosts" on the Hookup. Eight fifteen passed. And eight thirty . . .

The telephone rang. The first voice came over the speaker.

"Man on bicycle wearing helmet, goggles, earphone, and backpack on the 1400 block of Olive Street! A car window just smashed! I didn't see the man on the bicycle do anything!"

Pete was dismayed. "He didn't do anything!"

"No," Jupiter said, biting his lip, "but he was there."

The telephone rang again.

"On the 1300 block of Olive, the man on the bicycle just rode past and the front window of a gray Ford smashed! Biker did not stop."

"He didn't stop!" Paul cried.

"But the windows are breaking as he passes!" Bob said.

"Window on blue Mercedes shattered on 1200 block of Olive Street! Biker passed. Seemed to take something from under his shirt."

Paul said, "The patrolman I talked to said it looked

as if the man on the bike was going to take something from under his shirt!"

"But what?" Pete cried.

"Wait, let's listen!" Bob urged.

Jupiter said, "Nothing will happen for the next two or three blocks, Records. Watch!"

"Man wearing goggles and earphone and riding a ten-speed just passed through the 1100 block of Olive Street. Nothing happened at all!"

The others stared at Jupiter.

"Man on bicycle you described rode down the 1000 block of Olive, but nothing happened, guys!"

"How did you know!" Pete said to Jupiter.

"When I went to police headquarters on Friday, I asked Chief Reynolds where tonight's stakeout would be. He told me it would be on the 1000 block of Olive Street," Jupiter explained. "The smasher knew where the police were again!"

"On the 900 block of Olive Street. The man on the ten-speed just passed. I think maybe he took something from under his shirt and a Chevette side window smashed! Couldn't see anything else!"

"But what could he have under his shirt?" Bob asked. "I mean, that could break a car window?"

"If he throws something, why don't they see him do it?" Paul wondered. "They should see him throw something even at night."

"Guy on bike who looks like a spaceman on 800 block of Olive Street. Window on Cadillac smashed! He could have aimed something at the Caddy, fellows! I'm not sure. He's riding pretty fast and it's dark, but he could have aimed something!"

Bob turned to Pete. "Second, where's that small hunk of metal you found in Paul's panel truck?"

"Right here." Pete took the little lump of silvery metal out of his pocket and handed it to Bob.

"Of course!" Bob said, excited. "See those ridges? And how it used to be part hollow and part solid? I *thought* I knew what it was!"

"So what *is* it?" Pete demanded.

"An air-gun pellet!" Bob said, looking at his friends. "He's using an air gun to shoot out the car windows. A powerful one!"

"From the 700 block on Olive Street. The guy on the ten-speed in the helmet and all rode right past a green Mercury, and the window busted! I didn't see the biker do anything."

"I think you're right, Records!" Jupiter said, too elated to care that Bob had come up with the answer first. "All he has to do is slip the pistol out from under his shirt, aim quickly as he rides close by the car, and fire. It would only take seconds, make no sound, and hardly be noticeable as he rides past in the dark. And it would leave only a little lump of metal that no one would even find unless he was looking for it!"

"We'd better call the police!" Paul exclaimed. "Now my dad'll believe me."

"Yes," Jupiter agreed. "We'll . . . No, wait! We can't call the police yet! We must catch him our-selves!"

"Why, Jupe?" Pete wanted to know. "The chief said—"

"I'll explain later. Now we must—"

"Jupiter, Bob, Pete! The police have caught the man on the ten-speed breaking a window! They're holding him at the corner of Olive and Chapala streets! I'm going out there!"

"Let's go!" Bob urged.

"Bikes are too slow," Jupiter decided. "We'll get Hans or Konrad to drive us!"

They rushed out through Easy Three and ran to the salvage yard office. One of the two yard trucks was parked in front, but only Uncle Titus was in the office.

"I'm sorry, boys," Uncle Titus said. "Hans and Konrad went somewhere with Mathilda, and I'm waiting for a phone call."

"I can drive," Paul said. "I have my license with me."

"Can he, Uncle Titus?" Jupiter asked.

"Well, I don't see why not," Uncle Titus said.

Paul drove carefully through the deserted streets of the town to the corner of Olive and Chapala streets.

Excited, the boys looked around the intersection for the police and the captured bicyclist.

No one was there.

"I-I don't see anyone," Pete stammered.

The streets were empty as far as the boys could see. There was nothing to be seen or heard in the dark, silent night.

"There's no one here," Bob said, dismayed.

Paul said, "Jupiter? What—"

"A trick!" Jupiter suddenly cried. "We've been tricked, fellows. A wild-goose chase! That voice on the phone wasn't one of our Ghost-to-Ghost people!"

13
Defeat!

"But why, Jupe?" Pete said.

The Second Investigator was looking up and down the silent streets, his eyes searching for the swarm of policemen that should have been there arresting the guilty biker.

"To keep us from calling the police," Jupiter guessed, "or to get us away from Headquarters and the Ghost-to-Ghost reports! Quick, Paul, drive back along Olive Street! Maybe the man on the bike hasn't reached here yet. Maybe he's still riding along Olive."

Paul turned the truck onto Olive Street and drove slowly along the quiet residential blocks. The Three Investigators peered ahead for some sign of the man on the ten-speed.

"Look for broken car windows," Jupiter instructed.

"I've been looking, First," Bob replied. "So far I haven't seen any."

Paul continued along the street of old houses and parked cars as they all watched for broken windows and the helmeted cyclist.

"There!" Bob cried. "A broken car window!"

They had reached the 600 block of Olive Street.

"Stop the truck, Paul," Jupiter said.

Paul pulled to the curb beside a big parked Buick with a broken window next to the driver's seat. Jupiter stared ahead along the dim blocks of Olive Street.

"This is one block beyond where we heard the last report of a broken window," the First Investigator said. "It looks as if he broke one more window after we went out on our wild-goose chase, then stopped and disappeared between this block and the corner of Chapala."

"Gee, why, Jupe? I mean, what made him stop?" Pete wondered.

"Let's get back to Headquarters," Jupiter decided. "Maybe the Ghost-to-Ghost can tell us something."

Paul drove as fast as he could down the residential streets, back to the salvage yard on the outskirts of town. Once inside Headquarters, Jupiter activated the telephone answering machine and located the message that had sent them dashing off so hastily.

"*Jupiter, Bob, Pete! The police have caught the man on the ten-speed breaking a window! They're holding him at the corner of Olive and Chapala streets. I'm going out there!*"

The voice of the imposter stopped. The boys waited for the machine to continue with the next report.

"*From the 600 block of Olive Street. Your biker rode past a big Buick and the window smashed all over! But the guy didn't do anything. I mean, except maybe sort of point at the Buick.*"

"It must be real hard to see that air gun," Paul observed.

Jupiter nodded. "The biker rides quite fast, it's dark, and who thinks of a man on a bicycle as someone who would shoot out car windows? Anyone who hears, or even sees, the windows smash looks at the car first, and then the biker is already past and riding away. The air gun is hidden by his body and is probably back in his belt within seconds. Our kids only saw as much as they did because they were specifically watching for the biker."

"*On the 500 block of Olive, fellows. Your guy on the ten-speed rode by. At least he looked like the biker you described. But nothing happened! No window broke. Nothing.*"

"He was still on Olive," Paul exclaimed, "but not shooting!"

They waited for the next report. The answering machine remained silent. There were no more messages on the tape.

"That was it," Bob said. "He rode through the 500 block, and no one on the Ghost-to-Ghost saw him again!"

"What happened, Jupe?" Pete wondered. "We've got kids all over town on the Ghost-to-Ghost. Someone should have spotted him even if he wasn't breaking windows."

"Even if he turned off Olive Street," Paul said.

Jupiter bit his lower lip. "There are only two possible explanations. Either he took off all his equipment and abandoned his bicycle so our watchers wouldn't recognize him, or someone picked him up in a car or truck and drove him away."

"But why, Jupe?" Pete said. "You think he found out the Ghost-to-Ghost kids were watching him?"

"That," Jupiter said, "is exactly what I think happened."

"How?" Paul wanted to know.

"He was told he was being watched, Paul! He was warned, so he stopped shooting and vanished."

"Warned?" Paul said doubtfully.

"Perhaps someone on the Ghost-to-Ghost knew him and went out and warned him," Bob suggested.

Jupiter shook his head. "Not quite, fellows. It's all becoming clear. He knew about us the same way he always knew where the police were staked out to catch him. Someone warned him, all right—through his earphone!"

"His earphone?"

"Isn't that just attached to a radio in his backpack?"

"It must be a CB!"

"Or a ham radio!"

"At least a radio that receives police calls," Jupiter declared. "When I spoke to Chief Reynolds on Friday I asked if the stakeouts were in radio contact with headquarters and each other. He said of course they were. That's when I realized how the man on the bike always knew where the police were—he heard them on his radio tuned to the police wavelength. And that's how someone warned him tonight, I'm sure of it! Someone who used the same wavelength to warn him that the Ghost-to-Ghost was watching."

"But Jupe," Bob objected, his voice uneasy, "only the four of us knew about the Ghost-to-Ghost Hookup tonight."

"Right," Pete said. "How did that imposter who sent us on the wild-goose chase know about the Hookup? And how did he know what number to call?"

"I think I can show you," Jupiter said. "We'll need our high-beam flashlight and also the long ladder out in the workshop."

Minutes later the stout First Investigator was leading the others, who carried the heavy ladder, back to Red Gate Rover in the rear fence. Jupiter removed the latch behind the knothole and swung up the boards. Once outside the fence, he headed for the telephone pole with the wires going into the salvage yard.

"I want you to climb the ladder up to that telephone box on the pole, Pete," Jupiter instructed.

"What do I do when I get up there?"

"You open the box and tell us what you see."

With the flashlight slung over his shoulder on its cord, the athletic Second Investigator positioned the ladder securely against the pole and climbed up it. He opened the telephone box and shined the flashlight inside.

"All I see is a lot of wires. I mean, it looks . . . No, hold it. There *is* something here."

"What is it, Second?" Jupiter called up.

Pete peered closely into the box high on the telephone pole. "I don't know. Some kind of metal or plastic cube hooked up to a couple of terminals. I mean, it looks like it's hooked into the telephone lines. You want me to bring it down?"

"No!" Jupiter shouted up. "Don't touch it. Just come down."

On the ground Pete looked back up the pole. "It's a wiretap, isn't it? Hooked into our telephone line. That's how someone knew about the Ghost-to-Ghost and could cut into our line and give us the fake report."

Jupiter nodded. "It was the only answer when I thought about it all."

Bob stared up to the telephone box. "But where is he listening from? I don't see any wires leading out of the box except the regular telephone lines."

"It must be a special kind of remote listening device that sends its signals by radio," Jupiter decided. "We're dealing with someone who knows a great deal about electronics."

"Someone who's been keeping an eye on us all along," Bob said.

"You mean keeping an ear on us, don't you, Records?" Pete said, and grinned.

His pals stared at him, groaned, and walked back to Red Gate Rover, leaving Pete alone with the ladder.

"Hey, fellows, the ladder! Come on, it wasn't that bad!"

The others stopped and looked back at him.

"No more jokes?" Bob said.

"Okay, okay," Pete promised.

Laughing, the other three returned to help him with the ladder. Pete and Bob carried it back to the outdoor workshop, then crawled through Tunnel Two into the hidden trailer. They found Jupiter and Paul listening again to the telephone answering machine.

"Jupiter, Bob, Pete! The police have caught the man on the ten-speed breaking a window! They're

holding him at the corner of Olive and Chapala streets. I'm going out there!"

"Does anyone recognize the voice?" Jupiter asked.

"I'm not sure," Bob said. "There's something—"

"It sounds sort of disguised to me," Paul said.

"Maybe kind of Chinese?" Pete suggested.

"A little Oriental," Jupiter agreed, "like the voice the rental agency clerk described to Worthington. The person who called to ask about us after that first Monday. He was probably the intruder we chased last week, and I'll bet anything he was the telephone man Aunt Mathilda saw on the pole last Thursday. That's probably when he put in the wiretap."

"But who is he?" Pete exclaimed. "I mean, what does he want? Why is he watching us?"

"He must be the window smasher's partner or something," Paul suggested.

Jupiter chewed his lip. "They do appear to be working together."

"But what's the point of it all?" Bob said. "Why are they breaking the car windows? An air gun, electronics, a police-band radio, a wiretap? That's a pretty fancy setup just to break some windows."

"There has to be a good reason," Pete decided. "Something important the smasher gets out of it all, you know?"

"Maybe it really was just to steal old Jarvis Temple's coin," Paul said. "A coin worth two hundred and fifty thousand dollars is a pretty good reason."

"Jupe?" Bob said. "What do you think?"

The leader of the Investigators was sitting at his desk, once more studying the map with its rows of colored pushpins. He sighed.

"There is probably a reason we haven't figured out yet," he said, "but it doesn't really matter anymore. The case is over."

The other three boys stared at the First Investigator, speechless. Jupiter stared back at them all.

"He's gone," he said miserably. "We've lost our man."

In the hidden trailer all four boys just sat there.

"We know the man on the ten-speed is the window smasher," Jupiter went on, "but we don't know who he is! We don't know his name, or anything about him, or even what he looks like without his helmet and goggles. We never saw his face at all! And now he's gone. He knows he's been spotted, so he won't break any more windows."

Pete groaned. "Jupe's right. We know he's the smasher, but we can't catch him."

Jupiter nodded dismally. "We've solved the case, but we can't prove it to anyone."

The boys sat there doing nothing for another few minutes. Finally Pete looked at the clock.

"Well, it's late," he said. "I guess we'd better go home."

Bob nodded glumly. "We might as well. He sure won't break any more windows, so I guess the case *is* over."

"Now my dad will never believe me," Paul groaned.

14
Jupiter Strikes Back

At breakfast the next morning, Paul's father stared at him incredulously.

"A man on a ten-speed bicycle wearing a helmet, goggles, earphones, and a backpack? Shooting out car windows with an air pistol?"

"It's true, Dad! Jupiter and the guys proved it last night."

Paul told his father all about the biker and the Ghost-to-Ghost Hookup.

"Ghost-to-Ghost Hookup?" Mr. Jacobs' eyes glazed.

Paul described how the Ghost-to-Ghost had first proved to the boys that windows were being smashed all over Rocky Beach, not only on the panel truck, and how it had caught the biker in the act. His father began to nod approvingly as he listened, and the disbelief in his eyes was gradually replaced by admiration.

"My word, Paul, that's a really clever idea. Ghost-to-Ghost Hookup, hmm? A good name at that," Mr. Jacobs said, and laughed. "So, what explanation did this biking vandal give the police when they arrested him?"

"We . . . we haven't told the police yet."

"Haven't told the police?" Mr. Jacobs frowned. "Why not? You don't intend to try to capture him yourselves?"

"No, Dad," Paul said.

"What, then?"

"We . . . we don't know who he is," Paul said miserably. "I mean, we don't know his name, or where he lives, or what he looks like out of the helmet and goggles and biking outfit."

"You don't know who he is?" Mr. Jacobs blinked at his son.

"He got away before we could actually catch him, Dad! But we'll figure it out! I mean . . . somehow."

"I see," Mr. Jacobs said, and returned to his breakfast. "Come on, Paul, I know you want to drive the truck again, but really! You did a fine job watching the shop while I was away, but the truck remains off-limits until you tell me exactly how the windows were broken."

Disconsolately, Paul finished his breakfast. Then

he decided to ride his old bike to the salvage yard. Perhaps Jupiter, Bob, and Pete would have thought of some way to identify the man on the ten-speed, although he didn't see how. He'd tossed and turned all night, racking his brain, and hadn't come up with anything that would help solve their problem.

When Paul arrived at the salvage yard, he found Pete and Bob in the outdoor workshop.

"Where's Jupiter?"

"That's a good question," Pete said.

"He's not here, Paul," Bob explained. "We waited inside Headquarters for almost an hour, but he didn't show up."

"We went to the office, but only Konrad was there. He didn't know where Jupe was either," Pete said.

"He thought Jupe might have gone with Uncle Titus in the truck," Bob added.

"So we decided to wait out here," Pete said, shrugging. "It's too depressing in Headquarters. Looking at the map with all the pushpins, listening to that voice that sent us on the wild-goose chase and let the biker get away."

"Have either of you thought of any way we could still catch the man on the ten-speed?"

Both the junior detectives shook their heads unhappily. The three boys sat in the outdoor workshop in silence. A half hour passed, and still Jupiter did not appear. Then they saw the truck drive into the yard. They all stood waiting expectantly, but only Hans and Uncle Titus got out. The boys hurried to the office.

"Have you seen Jupe, Mr. Jones?" Bob asked.

"Not since last night, boys," Jupiter's uncle said. "He went to bed very depressed—didn't even eat his late-night snack! And this morning he was up and gone before I came down. I don't think he had any breakfast, either."

"No snack last night?" Bob wondered.

"No breakfast?" Pete echoed in disbelief.

"Where could he have gone?" Paul said.

"I don't know," Uncle Titus said, "but when you see him, please let us know. His aunt is a little worried."

The boys nodded and slowly walked back to the outdoor workshop.

"What could he be doing?" Paul said to the two Investigators.

"Maybe he just didn't want to be around Headquarters either," Bob said.

Pete nodded and sighed. Paul looked sadly toward the main gate, where Hans and Konrad were unloading Uncle Titus' latest purchases from the truck. Bob leaned glumly against a workbench.

Suddenly, out of nowhere, a voice said, "Are you three going to mope around out there doing nothing?

We've got work to do to solve this mystery! Do I have to wait all day for you?"

"Jupe!" Pete cried.

"Where is he?" Paul looked around the workshop.

"There!" Bob pointed to the intercom speaker Jupiter had hooked up. "He's inside the trailer! Come on!"

Bob and Pete started to crawl into Tunnel Two before they remembered that Paul might be too big to make it through. They backed out and all three boys ran around the junk to the old oak door of Easy Three. Pete used the rusty iron key to open the door, and soon they were hurrying through the old boiler and into Headquarters. Jupiter sat at the desk smiling smugly and looking benevolently at the map with its rows of colored pushpins.

"Where did you come from?" Bob demanded. "We've been waiting for you all morning!"

"Oh, I came in the back way," Jupe replied airily.

"Uncle Titus said you were depressed," Pete said accusingly. "But you don't look a bit depressed!"

"Depressed?" Jupiter chortled. "Why would I be depressed when we're about to solve what looked like the most hopeless case of our entire career!"

"How?" all three boys asked in unison.

Jupiter beamed maddeningly. "Actually, the solution was suggested by all of you last night, but I was too depressed to pay attention. It was only in the middle of the night, faint with hunger because I hadn't eaten my snack, that I finally realized what Bob had said and you'd all agreed with."

"What!" his listeners cried, exasperated.

"That we must find out *why* the biker broke the windows!" The First Investigator continued to beam at the other three boys. "You were right. All we have to do now is figure out why he smashed the windows and we'll know who he is."

The three listeners sat there silently. They looked at each other. Then they looked at Jupiter.

"I don't know, First," Bob said dubiously.

"Gee," Paul objected, "even if we knew why, there could be a whole lot of people with the same reason."

"No," Jupiter said firmly, "I think not, Paul. I think that once we know why the windows were smashed, we will have a very narrow area in which to look for the smasher."

"It seems shaky to me," Pete said, "but Jupe's always right, so let's give it a try. Why *did* the biker smash all those windows? Maybe because he hates windows!"

"Or cars," Bob said. "He likes to damage cars."

"No." Jupiter shook his head. "In that case I doubt he would have smashed only one window per block. He would have been more likely to smash all the windows he could in one place and disappear. Instead, what we have here is a careful plan to space out the smashed windows. I think the smasher was trying to avoid attention, to make each incident seem like a simple accident."

"Well, what about careful vandalism?" Paul suggested. "I mean, he enjoys busting windows, but still doesn't want to be caught."

"Vandals don't think their destruction out that carefully, Paul," Jupiter analyzed. "Vandalism is only hate. People feel injured, held down, cheated, or discriminated against by the world, and they want to get back at the world that's hurting them. Vandalism is usually quite spontaneous, committed in a rage, and therefore quite easy to spot."

"This sure isn't easy," Paul agreed.

"Correct, Paul." Jupiter nodded. "This smasher planned very carefully to hide what was happening and protect himself. It's really not satisfying to a vandal if no one knows what he's done. He may not want to be caught, but he does want people to know what he did and why."

"Okay," Bob said, "how about revenge, First?"

"On whom, Records?"

"The car manufacturers. Someone who got a lemon, so he hates Ford or Toyota or some other car company."

"Then wouldn't all the broken windows be on the same brand of car? It wouldn't make much sense to take revenge on a company that didn't manufacture the lemon. Besides, why just break a window? Why not do some more serious damage?"

"Anyway," Pete pointed out, "you'd want to wreck cars the company still owned, not those they'd already sold to people."

"Okay," Bob said, "maybe revenge on some car owners."

"Too many cars involved, Records. The biker couldn't have something against hundreds of people."

"How about a plain, ordinary, everyday nut," Pete tried.

"Boy, this biker didn't act like any nut," Paul said.

Pete sighed. "I suppose not."

"Jupe?" Bob said. "What about the double eagle after all? Maybe the whole scheme *was* to cover up that single theft. You know, break all those windows to hide the fact that he really only wanted to break one special window and steal the eagle."

Jupiter nodded thoughtfully. "I considered that very carefully, but the fact that nothing else was stolen seems to rule it out. If you want to hide a criminal purpose among many of the same acts, you have to do the same things. To hide a theft that way, you'd need many *thefts*, not many broken windows. As it is, the one theft stands out."

"Well, then . . ." Pete thought hard.

"Could it be that—" Paul began.

"Maybe," Bob interrupted, then stopped and shook his head. "I can't think of another reason, First."

"I'm sure we all could if we really worked on it, but I don't think we have to. There are many possibilities, but only one really probable reason—as Pete pointed out last night."

"Me?" Pete wondered. "When did I do that?"

"When you said there had to be something the smasher *gained* from smashing the windows. Fellows, who profits from broken car windows?"

The three others blinked at Jupiter.

"Profits?" Paul said. "Who can profit from a broken window?"

Pete almost shouted, "The people who make the windows!"

"No," Bob cried, "not *make* the windows, *fix* the windows! The people who replace the broken glass."

"Exactly, Records." Jupiter beamed. "The people who replace the glass in the cars are the only ones who could really profit from the smashed windows."

Paul, who had been frowning, said, "But Jupiter, almost all service stations and body shops will fix broken car windows. How much profit is there for all of them?"

"That had me stumped for a while, too," Jupiter agreed. "So I got up early this morning and went to visit several service stations and repair shops. I asked them where they got the glass to fix car windows. A few send to Los Angeles or directly to the car manufacturers, but most told me they get their glass locally. And fellows, there is only one company in Rocky Beach that sells replacement windows for all makes of car—Margon Glass Company!"

15
Who Is the Smasher?

Margon Glass Company consisted of a one-story yellow brick building and three corrugated-metal warehouse buildings behind it, all surrounded by a six-foot wire fence. The place was on the outskirts of Rocky Beach, less than a mile from the salvage yard. There was a side gate for delivery trucks and employees, and a front gate for visitors to the office and retail store. Two loading docks stuck out behind the yellow building and the employee parking spaces next to them were half empty. The customer parking lot to the right of the main building was constantly busy.

"You think the smasher is the owner of the company?" Bob asked.

"Not necessarily, Records," Jupiter said.

Hidden in tall brown wild oats, the four boys lay

on a low hill that overlooked the road and Margon's fenced yard and buildings. Their bicycles were locked up at the base of the hill, on the side away from the road.

"It could be a salesman who wants larger commissions," Jupiter continued, watching the activity below, "or perhaps a new sales manager wants to look good. Or some employee is afraid he might be let go if business falls off."

"Then how do we find him," Paul wanted to know, "when we don't know what he looks like?"

"We know he's tall and thin and probably young— you don't see many older people decked out in biking outfits and riding ten-speeds. There can't be too many Margon people who fit that description."

From their vantage point on top of the hill, the boys watched the company for over an hour. The main building opened not onto the road but onto the customer parking lot to the right. A steady stream of cars pulled into and out of the lot.

"Why so many customers at a wholesale glass company?" Pete wondered.

"There's no such thing as a simple wholesale glass company anymore," Paul explained. "Everyone sells all kinds of extra stuff these days. Lumber companies have hardware departments, paint companies are like department stores. You can get all sorts of house things at Margon—you know, windows, mirrors, ladders, lamps, like that."

The long front wall of the main building held a row of large windows, opening into an office area. The boys could see people working at desks and standing before filing cabinets. In the rear yard two men were unloading a large truck and carrying big, flat boxes into a warehouse. Several times a short man came from the back of the main building, entered one of the three warehouses, and returned with a thin, flat, brown-paper package that clearly contained a single pane of some type of glass.

"Gee," Paul said, "none of those men look like the biker."

"No, they don't," Jupiter admitted. "He's got to be in the store or the office or back in a warehouse. Or he could be a salesman. There are probably wholesale salesmen who are out selling now."

After a while, the large truck drove out of the yard with one of the two men driving. The other man began to load a panel truck and a special glass-carrying truck with high, sloping sides against which very large pieces of plate glass could be carried vertically. The man used a forklift truck to bring the flat boxes from the warehouse buildings to the trucks. For the extra-large sheets of glass he called the short man from the main building, and they carried individually wrapped pieces to the special truck by hand.

"What do we do, Jupe?" Bob asked. "Watch and wait?"

"No, I just wanted to ascertain the pattern of movement down there," the First Investigator replied. "The large truck was obviously delivering glass from the manufacturer. The panel truck and that special glass truck must deliver to local repair shops and builders. I assume they'll depart soon. Occasionally that short guy brings a piece of glass from a warehouse to the store, but not often enough to serve the large number of customers we've seen come and go. I take that to mean most of the small stock is kept handy in the main building. We haven't seen anyone come out of a warehouse to help, so probably there's no one back in there. Do we all agree with my observations?"

"Sounds right to me, First," Pete said.

The other two boys nodded.

"Good," Jupiter said crisply. "Then I suggest we wait until the panel truck and the special truck go to make their deliveries. That should leave the warehouse area deserted, with only a small chance that an employee will come into it. Paul and I will go into the store and try to observe who is working there and in the office, while Pete and Bob sneak around to the rear and search the warehouse area for any evidence of our biker. In the store, Paul and I will try to keep everyone busy to cover Pete and Bob."

"How come Bob and I always do the sneaking around?" Pete demanded.

"I thought it best to have a licensed driver ask about car-window glass," Jupiter said somewhat stiffly. "And as I am by far the best actor, I am the logical choice to keep the people in the store occupied."

Bob grinned. "He's right, Pete."

"As usual." Pete sighed.

The man on the forklift continued to load both trucks for another half hour. Then he climbed into the panel truck and drove it out of the yard, leaving the side gate open. Moments later the short man who had been helping him came out of the main building, got into the special glass truck, and followed the panel truck out through the open gate.

The entire warehouse area was now deserted.

"All right, Records and Second," Jupiter said. "Remember, we may be dealing with a dangerous thief. If you find any proof that our biker is here, signal by chalking a large question mark on the front of the smallest warehouse. Paul and I will go back to Headquarters at once and call Chief Reynolds while you remain to watch the evidence."

Bob and Pete went down the reverse slope of the low hill and circled around to reach the open gate in the fence on the side street. Paul and Jupiter slipped down the hill through the wild oats and casually sauntered across the road, through the main gate, and into the Margon Glass Company store.

Four customers stood at the shop counter attended by three clerks. Behind the counter, shelves loaded with house glass and hardware items vanished into the depths of the building. All around the shop were window frames, mirrors, decorative glass, and wrought-iron accessories. On the right, a window in the customer area looked out on the warehouse yard. On the left, a glass partition that ran the length of the building separated the company offices from the store. Three women and four men were visible in the offices.

Jupiter and Paul stood behind the one waiting customer and studied the company personnel. Of the three salesclerks, one was a plump older man, one was tall and thin but not young, and the third was a tall, thin, athletic-looking young man. Paul nudged Jupiter and nodded toward the young salesman. Jupiter studied him thoughtfully.

The customer ahead of them took his turn at the counter.

Through the glass partition Jupiter could see that the three women in the office were all young, but only one was slender and she was no taller than five-foot-five. Of the four men, one was tall, middle-aged, and sitting alone in a private office with the name J. Margon, President, on the door. Two others were young office clerks, neither of them tall. And the fourth, though tall and thin, was an old man who sat at a larger desk and watched everyone else closely— the office manager.

"Jupiter!"

It was Paul's voice whispering in alarm. Another one of the clerks at the counter had become free, but instead of waiting on Jupe and Paul, he was walking toward the side door that led into the rear yard!

16
A Close Call

When they saw Paul and Jupiter cross the street, Bob and Pete waited another two minutes at the side gate and then hurried through into the warehouse area. No one was around. There was only one window in the rear wall of the main building, up in the store area, and all the doors and loading dock gates were closed.

The two boys slipped into the first warehouse.

It was a one-story corrugated-steel structure. In its dim interior loomed long rows of shelves that held wooden boxes of plate glass and tall racks filled with large sheets wrapped in heavy brown paper. Bob and Pete listened to be sure they were alone. There was only a motionless silence.

The boys moved quickly along the rows of shelves,

searching for any sign of the window-smashing biker. There were few hiding places in the building. The walls were bare and the long rows of shelves stacked full.

Bob looked under all the shelves and Pete checked behind each rack. They found nothing. At the rear of the building a small office was partitioned off. It was being used now as only another storage area for wooden boxes of heavy glass. A single closet in the office was empty.

Returning to the front of the warehouse, the two Investigators peered carefully out into the deserted yard. They could hear the cars coming and going in the customers' parking lot out front, but no cars or trucks entered the warehouse area.

"All clear," Pete said.

They hurried across the open space between buildings.

"Pete!" Bob gasped.

The door from the main building into the yard was opening!

Jupiter stepped quickly to the end of the counter where the clerk was about to go out the door and into the yard.

"My good man, I believe we are next. My business is quite urgent. Time is money."

The clerk pushed the door open. "I'll be right back, kid."

"A kid, my man, is a young goat," Jupiter snapped. "I prefer to be referred to as 'sir.' And it is imperative that I procure a new window for my Rolls-Royce so that Paul there can have it installed at once and drive me immediately to Los Angeles. If you are too busy to serve me, perhaps I should speak to the owner of this enterprise?"

His hand on the knob of the half-open door, the clerk hesitated.

"Come, come," Jupiter said haughtily, "shall I speak to the owner? A Mr. Margon, correct? I do believe Father does business with Mr. Margon, does he not, Paul?"

His round face at its most smug and aloof, the stout Investigator looked toward Paul, who was trying to keep from laughing. The older boy quickly wiped any hint of a smile from his face and joined in the charade.

"I believe he does, Master Jones," he said in an almost perfect imitation of Worthington.

This was too much for the clerk. He closed the door and returned behind the counter to face Jupiter.

"Er," the clerk said, "I'm not sure we have Rolls-Royce windows."

"Surely you jest!" Jupiter's round face was a picture of complete astonishment.

The nervous clerk paled. "Well, maybe we do. I'll check in back."

"If you would be so kind." Jupiter beamed benevolently. "The model is a 1937 Silver Cloud."

The clerk gulped, nodded, and went back into the rows of shelves at the rear, mumbling the model name to himself.

Caught between buildings in the bright sunlight, Bob and Pete stood frozen as the door from the main building seemed to remain open for an eternity.

Then it slowly closed.

"Whew," Pete breathed.

"Come on," Bob urged. "Let's get to the next warehouse before someone really does come out!"

They quickly covered the remaining open space between the buildings. In the half-light of the interior, the second warehouse was laid out exactly like the first, with shelves and racks fading away to the rear. But here the shelves and racks held framed windows, mirrors, glass doors, wall panels, and other special glass items.

The two boys repeated their search among the racks and shelves. Again they found nothing. Back at the entrance they peered out, saw no one, and, keeping their eyes on the door from the main building, ran across the sun-glare of the open space to the third

and smallest warehouse. Here in the shadowy interior the shelves that lined the walls were loaded with
all the accessories for windows and glass doors, mirrors, and glass panels. In the center, a long workbench contained glass-cutting and mounting tools.

Bob worked his way to the rear along the left shelves,
Pete along the right. They found nothing of interest.
The partitioned office at the back was crammed with
tall cardboard cartons of housekeeping supplies—paper
towels, liquid soap, toilet tissue, paper cups, coffee
filter papers, and plastic cups.

"Records!"

Pete had found a canvas tarpaulin over some boxes
at the rear of the small office. He lifted it up. Under
it a ten-speed bicycle leaned against the wall.

"Is it his?" the Second Investigator wondered.

"I can't tell for sure." Bob hesitated. "It was so
dark those two nights we saw him, I couldn't make
out the color."

"The seat's the right height for a tall man—all the
way up," Pete decided.

The Second Investigator stepped back to get a better view, leaned against one of the big boxes of paper
towels, and almost fell over as the box slid away from
under him. Bob stared at the still-rocking carton.

"That's awfully light for a carton of paper towels,"
he said. "But it looks like there's *something* inside
it. Let's check."

They opened the box. Inside they found a helmet, a pair of goggles, a backpack with a radio, an earphone, a yellow biking shirt, black biker tights, and biking shoes.

Jupiter maintained his arrogant demeanor at the shop counter as the salesclerk returned.

"No Rolls-Royce glass," the clerk announced. "We can get it for you, but it'll take two weeks."

"That is preposterous!" Jupiter cried. "Quite out of the question. The repair shop must have it at once, which is why I have come to you myself."

"Sorry," the clerk said, and grinned, his confidence returning now that he could refuse a customer. "Two weeks on order."

At the window Paul stiffened.

"Ju—er, Master Jones!"

Jupiter sauntered casually to the side where Paul stood staring out the window into the company yard. On the front window of the small warehouse he saw a large chalked question mark!

"Well," he announced to the room in general, "we will have to go to Los Angeles without a window. The air might do me good, eh? Come, Paul."

Without another glance at the gaping clerks and customers, Jupiter grinned and stalked off with Paul behind him.

Once outside, the grin faded from the stout First

Investigator's face. He and Paul raced across the street and around the base of the hill to retrieve their bikes, then pedaled off toward the salvage yard to call Chief Reynolds.

Bob and Pete crouched at the front window of the small warehouse. Some ten minutes had passed since they'd chalked their question mark to announce their find.

"It shouldn't take much more than half an hour," Bob calculated. "About ten minutes to ride to the salvage yard, maybe ten to tell Chief Reynolds all about it, and ten or fifteen minutes for the police to get here."

"I wish we could capture him ourselves," Pete said.

"We solved the case," Bob said. "And this guy might be dangerous. Don't forget, we didn't find his pistol."

"I still wish—" Pete began.

Just then, a honey-colored Corvette came through the open side gate with a squeal of tires and swerved violently into one of the empty parking spaces behind the main building. A young man jumped out and strode across the pavement.

"Look, Second!" Bob whispered.

The young man was tall and thin. His pale face was framed by long dark hair down to the collar of his blue sport coat. He had a thin nose and a thin, greedy mouth. There was a nervousness about his eyes, but in slim gray slacks and short black boots he swaggered toward the main building as if he owned it.

"He sure fits Jupe's idea of what the biker should look like," Bob exclaimed softly.

They watched the young man march on into the main building. Pete looked at his watch.

"We'd better get his license number," he said. "He could leave again before they get here."

The Second Investigator was still writing down the number when the rear door was flung open and the skinny young man darted out of the store. He hurried across the yard straight toward the warehouse where Pete and Bob were crouched at the window.

"He's coming here!"

The two boys looked for cover.

"Bottom shelf!"

Near the door, the bottom shelf had some empty space behind a large carton. The two boys crawled in.

The door opened with a crash. The young man ran through to the rear. The Investigators could hear him breathing hard. When he reappeared he had the biking helmet on his head, the goggles around his neck, the clothes stuffed into the backpack, and the pack dangling from the handlebars of the bike he was pushing out the door.

"He's got all the evidence!" Pete whispered fiercely.

"If he destroys it, we'll never prove he's the smasher!"

"We can't stop him, Second. It's too dangerous!"

But Pete was already crawling from their hiding place. Bob followed his friend to the front window.

"He's loading the stuff into his car."

Outside, the pale young man was struggling frantically to fit the ten-speed into his Corvette.

"He doesn't look dangerous to me," Pete said.

Before Bob could protest again, Pete was up and out the door and heading straight for the sports car. When the frantic young man saw Pete, he dropped the bicycle and dove into his car. Pete started to run.

The young man turned with a big, deadly looking gun in his hand. It was aimed directly at Pete.

17
A Smasher Caught!

Jupiter and Paul walked up and down in front of the salvage yard, staring along the street in both directions. After seeing the chalked question mark signal, they had ridden to the junkyard as fast as they could and called Chief Reynolds. Quickly, they filled him in on all that had happened since they had last talked.

"Margon Glass Company?" the chief had said over the telephone. "That's almost impossible to believe, Jupiter. I know Jim Margon personally."

"I'm afraid we have proof, sir. Bob and Pete are waiting now at the Margon warehouse with it."

"We'll pick you two up at the yard on our way."

Now Jupiter waited outside the gates with Paul, pacing nervously. Every few seconds he checked his watch.

"You think maybe Bob and Pete are in danger, Jupiter?" Paul said uneasily.

"There is always danger," Jupiter said grimly, "when you are protecting evidence. Especially when a quarter of a million dollars is involved."

At that moment three police cars turned the corner. In the first of the three, Chief Reynolds pulled up in front of the gates, and the boys climbed in. They drove off toward Margon Glass Company.

"You're sure about this, Jupiter?" the chief asked, his voice serious. "Someone at Margon Glass is behind all the smashed windows?"

"When you analyze it carefully, Chief, it's the only answer that makes sense," Jupiter explained quietly. "They are the one firm in Rocky Beach that sells replacement car windows, the only people who profit from every smashed window."

"I can't believe Jim Margon would do such a thing."

"It's possible this is being done without Mr. Margon's knowledge, sir. In fact, I'd be willing to bet that Mr. Margon knows nothing about it. It would be far too risky for him to try to build business that way."

"I hope you're right, Jupiter," Chief Reynolds said. "We're nearly there."

The chief spoke into his radio, and all the police cars slowed as they neared the Margon Company buildings.

"The side gate is open, Chief," Jupiter said.

Chief Reynolds nodded and directed his men to turn into the side street. As they did, a long, honey-colored sports car came careening wildly out of the side gate toward them. The driver jammed on his brakes and slewed to a stop, backed up in a scream of tires and a stink of burning rubber, then raced off in the other direction. At the same time, Bob came running out of the side gate. When he saw the police cars, he waved wildly.

"He's got Pete! In the car!"

Chief Reynolds barked over his radio, "Stop that Corvette!"

The police started after the small car—right down a dead-end street! The Corvette screeched to a stop just at the barrier. A tall young man with scared eyes and a blue blazer leaped from the car. He ran past the barrier into open fields crisscrossed by the deep gullies called barrancas.

"Stop him!" Chief Reynolds ordered.

"If he gets to that first barranca, we might never catch him!" Jupiter cried.

But the police were still too far from the end of the street.

"He's going to get away!" Paul wailed.

But another figure had hurtled out of the Corvette and was racing off in hot pursuit of the fleeing man. It was Pete! He gained rapidly as the two ran across the open fields toward the first barranca. Just as the police reached the barrier and started out over the fields, Pete flung himself at the running man and sent him sprawling with a magnificent open field tackle!

Instantly, the tall young man was on his feet again, but Pete clung doggedly to one leg. The man tried to shake his pursuer off, but as soon as he freed one leg Pete grabbed the other and hung on. They were still struggling toward the barranca when the police swarmed over them. Pete let go and lay on the grass, grinning up at everyone.

"There's your window smasher," he said.

The young man struggled in the hands of the police.

"I don't know what this is all about, but you'll all be sorry! Who are these kids? You're the police—arrest them!"

"Take a look back in his car, Chief," Pete said, getting up.

The young man began to swear as they dragged him back to the barrier, where Bob was standing beside the Corvette.

"Open the door, Records," Pete said.

They all saw the ten-speed bicycle jammed into the back; the helmet, goggles, and backpack with its radio and earphone; and the biking clothes spilling out of the backpack.

"They put all that in my car!" the young man cried. "It's a frame-up!"

"We have witnesses, including your own officers, who saw him pass stakeouts and broken windows," Jupiter said, "and you'll find all that equipment belongs to him. The bicycle has a police registration sticker, which I'm certain will prove to be in his name."

"Anyway," Pete said, "if you look under the front seat you'll find his air gun where he tried to hide it. I'll bet you can prove it belongs to him, and it sure must have his fingerprints on it."

The chief looked carefully under the seat. He brought out the odd-looking pistol, using a handkerchief to keep his own fingerprints off it. He held the pistol by the tip of its thick barrel and slipped it into a plastic evidence bag. The Investigators examined it curiously. Made of heavy blued steel, it resembled a real automatic but had a long rod on top of the heavy barrel, like a thinner second barrel. It weighed over two pounds, and "THE WEBLEY PREMIER—Made in England" was engraved on the barrel.

"A twenty-two-caliber air pistol," Chief Reynolds said. "That rod on top is for cocking the spring that compresses the air to fire it. A well-made pistol, large enough to smash any window at fairly close range." He nodded to his men. "Bring the suspect along.

We'll go and talk to Jim Margon about this. Now, boys, I want you to tell me exactly what happened here."

As they walked back toward Margon Glass Company, Bob explained how he and Pete had found the equipment and the bicycle hidden in the warehouse, how the young man had tried to remove it all and escape, and how Pete had confronted him.

"I guess I was crazy," Pete admitted, "but he just didn't look that dangerous to me. More like a scared kid. So I went out. He saw me and grabbed that air pistol. He held it on me and made me load the bike in the car and get in myself. He drove off still holding the pistol on me. But then he saw you and panicked, I guess. He must have forgotten about the dead end, and you saw the rest."

"You were lucky," Chief Reynolds said grimly. "An air pistol is no toy. It could kill you if fired at close range."

A small group of people from Margon Glass had gathered at the side gates. As the police walked through into the yard, one of the watchers ran back into the building. Soon the middle-aged man Jupiter and Paul had seen inside in the private office pushed through the people.

"William!" he cried. "What's going on here?"

The chief said, "You know this young man, Jim?"

"Oh, Chief, I didn't see you," Mr. Margon said. "Know him? Of course I know him. He's my son. Came back from college and joined the company a year ago. Been doing fine, too. Why are your men holding him? Who are these boys?"

The chief pointed to the bicycle being pushed by one of his men. "Is that your son's bicycle, Jim? His helmet, goggles?"

"Dad!" William Margon cried. "Don't—!"

"Bicycle?" Mr. Margon frowned at the ten-speed. "Yes, he rides with a bicycle club every Monday and Wednesday night at some indoor track. But he keeps all his equipment at home, not here at the yard. What's all this doing here, William?"

William Margon only glared at his father.

"I'm afraid I have bad news for you, Jim," the chief said, and he told Mr. Margon the whole story of the air pistol and the smashed car windows.

"Smashing car windows?" Mr. Margon said, his voice full of disbelief. "Why I . . . I made him sales manager of car windows only three months ago. He's done a great job. We've had more business than we ever did before. He . . ." Mr. Margon paused as he stared at his son. "You broke all those extra windows yourself?"

"They're lying, Dad! I don't know what they're talking about! It's all circumstantial! Someone stole my bike and equipment and then put it here! Maybe those kids did it themselves. Nobody can prove I broke any windows. No one ever saw my face!"

"We'll prove it for sure when we find out what you did with the stolen eagle!" Bob said hotly.

Mr. Margon blinked. "He stole an eagle?"

"Not the bird, sir," Bob explained, "a rare coin. Actually, the one your son stole after he broke a car window was a double eagle, an American twenty-dollar gold piece from 1907. It's worth two hundred and fifty thousand dollars, and he—"

"Two hundred and fifty thousand dollars?" Mr. Margon said, his voice shaking.

William Margon went pale. "You can't pin that on me! I never heard of a double eagle. Okay, I admit I broke all those windows. But I was just trying to build business. I never stole any coin!"

Jupiter, who had been silent ever since Bob and Pete had told them about finding William Margon's equipment, suddenly spoke up.

"No," he said, "I don't think you did."

18
The Copycat

Bob, Pete, and Paul all gaped at Jupiter. Bob found his voice first.

"He *didn't* steal the eagle, Jupe?"

"Jupiter?" Chief Reynolds said, his eyebrow raised. "Do you know something we don't?"

"I hope so, sir," Jupiter said slowly, "but I'm not absolutely certain."

"In something so serious," Chief Reynolds said, "you must be certain, Jupiter."

"I'm certain now that the biker didn't steal the eagle, sir. What I'm not sure of is exactly who did. But if you'll let me try, Chief, I think I can find out."

The chief shook his head. "I want to know how you came to this remarkable conclusion. Especially since you suggested all along that the thief and the smasher were the same person."

"No, sir, I don't believe I ever suggested that. We all simply assumed it to be the case, especially with Jarvis Temple making such a fuss. Now I think there's another explanation."

"What explanation, First?" Pete demanded.

"That we have a 'copycat' crime," Jupiter declared.

"A what crime?" Paul frowned.

Chief Reynolds said, "When there is a series of identical crimes obviously committed by one criminal, sometimes an entirely different criminal tries to make his crime look like one of the series so that the original criminal will be blamed for it too."

Jupiter nodded. "I think someone who knew about the broken windows took advantage of the situation to smash Sarah Temple's car window and steal the double eagle, hoping it would be blamed on the person smashing all the other windows."

"That's a lot of speculation, Jupiter," said Chief Reynolds.

"Perhaps, sir," Jupiter acknowledged, "but I became convinced of it when Pete told us about William Margon running out of the office and straight to the warehouse to move his bike and equipment to some other location."

Jupiter continued: "Almost from the start there has been someone else involved in the case, someone most concerned about Pete, Bob, and myself. Whoever it is first attempted to learn what we were doing by sneaking into the salvage yard and listening to us with some kind of microphone. When that failed, a wiretap was installed in our telephone line. That's how the person was able to warn William Margon that the Ghost-to-Ghost was watching him, and to send us on the wild-goose chase so that Margon could escape."

"But aren't they partners, Jupe?" Pete objected.

Jupiter shook his head. "Now that we have captured the smasher, it seems clear that he was acting alone to create business for Margon Glass. The other person wasn't trying to protect the smasher but to protect himself! The copycat didn't want the window smasher captured because then the police would be bound to learn that the smasher didn't steal the eagle."

"You're sure of this, Jupiter?" Chief Reynolds said doubtfully.

"Yes, Chief. In fact, I think the copycat called once more to warn young Margon in the hope of protecting himself." Jupiter turned to William Margon. "Am I right?"

The young man was staring at Jupiter. "How did you know?"

"Then you *were* called a little while ago and told that your hidden equipment had been discovered and the police were coming?"

Young Margon nodded. "The same voice that warned

me over my radio on the bike to get off Olive Street."

"High but muffled?" Jupiter said. "Hoarse, slightly Oriental-sounding?"

William Margon only nodded this time, dumbfounded.

"And you have no idea who it is?"

"No, none."

Chief Reynolds nodded slowly. "There *was* a report about a strange message on the police band last night. Something about being spotted and getting off Olive. You're right, Jupiter, there *is* someone else involved. What do you propose to do?"

Jupiter thought. "Whoever we're looking for has a great deal of knowledge about electronics and operates a radio transmitter. We could try to find out who fits that description, but there's a simpler way. I think I can deliver the thief by this evening, if you'll give me the afternoon to make my plans."

"Very well," the chief agreed. Turning to Mr. Margon and his son, he said, "I'm afraid we have to take William downtown now, Jim."

Mr. Margon nodded unhappily, looking at his son. "You may not be an outright thief, William, but you have committed serious acts of vandalism. How could a son of mine do such a thing? Whatever possessed you?"

"I just wanted to build the business, Dad, and make a lot of money."

"There are more important things than money, William."

"I wanted to be the best sales manager. I wanted to succeed! What's wrong with that?"

"Nothing, son," Mr. Margon said sadly, "except that *how* you succeed is more important than how *much* you succeed. Making money is only part of the goal."

"I . . . I just wanted to make you proud of me."

"No, I fear you just wanted to impress me. You wanted to succeed for all the wrong reasons, son. You wanted to be important, not do important things. Well, now you'll have to pay the price."

Chief Reynolds nodded, and the police led William Margon off to a patrol car. His father watched the young man go.

"Will he face criminal charges, Chief?" asked Mr. Margon.

"There will have to be an inquiry," Chief Reynolds said. "But if restitution is made, and we talk to a judge, I think probation might be arranged."

The Three Investigators and Paul left the two men talking. Crossing the street and skirting around the low hill, they retrieved the two remaining bikes and headed back to the salvage yard.

After dinner Jupiter sat alone in the hidden trailer room talking into the telephone.

"Second? Get Records and Paul and meet me here at Headquarters! I know now who stole the double eagle!"

"The double eagle?" Pete said from the other end. "You're sure it wasn't that guy on the bike the police arrested? That William Margon?"

"No, Second, it wasn't. I'm convinced this was a copycat crime, and now I know who did the copycatting."

"Who, Jupe?" Pete said eagerly.

"I'd rather show you the proof," Jupiter said maddeningly, "and let the three of you tell me if it isn't conclusive. I have the proof in the outdoor workshop. Meet me there in half an hour, and when I've shown you who the thief is, we'll take the proof to Chief Reynolds."

"Can't you give me a hint, Jupe?" Pete pleaded.

Jupiter gave a rather smug laugh. "Let us simply say that our copycat made one small but basic error."

With that, the First Investigator hung up. But he did not leave the hidden room. Instead, he sat humming softly to himself, glancing every now and then at his watch. His bright eyes glowed with eagerness and excitement. The ninth time he looked at his watch, he spoke aloud to the empty room.

"Time, Watson! The game's afoot!"

He opened the trap door down into Tunnel Two,

and, careful to make no sound, he crawled slowly to the mouth of the pipe where it opened into the out-door workshop.

There he lay motionless, no more than a shadow in the pipe, watching the silent workshop as twilight stole over Rocky Beach.

19
A Thief Unmasked!

The first faint sound came from the rear of the salvage yard near Red Gate Rover. Crouched at the shadowed mouth of Tunnel Two, Jupiter listened.

It could have been the sound of a climbing hook catching the overhang of the fence again. Then, vaguely, light steps over the metal of the overhang, and a distant soft thump of something dropping to the ground.

Jupiter waited patiently.

The second sound was a rattle of tin as if someone had bumped into the pile of roof gutters and downspouts stacked a few yards in from the rear fence. Someone was taking a slow, cautious path toward the workshop where Jupiter waited.

The third sound was a thump and a muffled cry of

pain from an entirely different direction—from somewhere near the open end of the workshop where a large stack of heavy lumber stood between the workshop and the salvage yard gates.

Jupiter groaned inwardly and held his breath. Had the cry carried to the back fence? He listened harder, straining to hear any new sounds.

For what seemed like an eternity there was only silence. Nothing but the distant sound of voices in the twilight and the far-off hum of traffic on the Coast Highway. The First Investigator chewed on his lower lip.

Then he heard a soft creak of wood just beyond the entrance to the workshop! Someone was climbing on the stack of old doors there. Climbing up to survey the workshop from above.

Jupiter waited inside the dark pipe.

The last sound was a light thud and soft footsteps almost on top of him!

Slowly he became aware of, rather than saw, a black shadow standing in the workshop no more than five feet from the mouth of Tunnel Two. Jupiter held his breath again.

A shadow that listened. Wary. A dark shape that must have come over the mound of junk and down into the empty workshop.

Jupiter waited.

The shadow moved and a tiny beam of light darted

around the workshop, searching the bench and shelves.

As the shadowy figure moved away from the entrance of Tunnel Two, it entered an area of brighter twilight. Now Jupiter could see the figure more clearly. It was a person dressed all in black: slim black jeans, a black sweatshirt, a tight black ski hood, black gloves, and black running shoes.

The hidden First Investigator watched the figure move slowly around the workshop, searching with the narrow beam of a pencil flashlight in the dusk. There was something familiar about the way the shape moved. Something . . . Suddenly Jupe knew the answer.

"Sarah Temple, I presume?"

The figure whirled and almost dropped the flashlight. From the narrow opening in the black ski hood, dark eyes flashed at the stout First Investigator as he emerged from the pipe.

Jupiter's voice was pleasant. "I really should have guessed from the start. When your uncle said he couldn't stand your fast driving or your CB radio. Your car would be that small red Datsun we saw in your driveway, the car you used the first time you came here to the yard. The satellite dish is yours too. You'd be a radio and TV nut as well as an electronics expert—you probably have a ham radio. Something of a rock climber and skier too, judging from the climbing hook and that hood you're hiding behind."

"I . . . I'm not hiding." Sarah Temple pulled off the hood, shook out her long dark hair. "I just came to talk to you about my uncle. I like wearing the hood. My uncle's changed his mind. He wants to hire you. He—"

"Ah, yes," Jupiter said imperturbably, "it would have been you who put your cousin Willard up to making that telephone call and inviting us over to talk about your uncle's coin. You needed a call while you were on the telephone pole, pretending to be a telephone man, so you could locate the correct line at the box. And of course you wanted us out of the way while you installed the wiretap itself."

"You must be crazy! What wiretap?"

"The wiretap," Jupiter said quietly, "that brought you here now to get the proof that you stole the double eagle." He watched the girl. "You could have known about the proof *only* by hearing me tell Pete about it on the telephone!"

Sarah Temple stood for a time looking silently at the stout leader of the detective team. Her face was pale in the fading twilight. "All right, I heard you talking on the phone. Where is it? The proof? Give me that proof!"

"I really should have known," Jupiter continued blandly. "*You* drove your uncle that night, and only *you* knew he had left the coin in the car. Anyone looking in would only have seen just a tiny box. You

knew about the smashed windows from hearing the
police on your radio. You must make a hobby of
listening to police calls. So you saw your chance to
grab the eagle and blame it on the window smasher.
A copycat theft."

"It's mine!" the tall girl cried. "I needed the money!
He never gives me enough money. I'll share it with
you, Jones! Fifty thousand dollars for you! Just give
me the proof, and you'll be rich."

Jupiter sighed in the growing dark. "You saw us
on your street around the Rolls. We acted oddly. You
became alarmed. We didn't alarm the police, but you
were nervous. What were we doing? So you disguised
your voice, traced us through the car-rental agency,
and tried to eavesdrop on us with one of your microphones. But you failed. Then, when you met us
two nights later and learned who we were and what
we were doing, you put in your wiretap to keep track
of our investigation. The one thing you had to prevent
was the capture of the window smasher and the dis-
covery that he had *not* stolen the double eagle."

"All right," Sarah Temple said. "Fifty-fifty! When
I sell the eagle, you get a hundred and twenty-five
thousand dollars!"

Jupiter shook his head. "You know, if you hadn't
made one small mistake at the start, you might have
gotten away with it."

"You can be rich! You can have everything you ever wanted!"

"No, Miss Temple," Jupiter said. "Not everything can be bought."

"Give me that proof!"

The tall girl took a step toward the stout First Investigator. Jupiter stood firm and looked her straight in the eye.

"There is no proof," he said.

"Liar!" She blinked at him. "No proof?"

"It was all a trap. I was certain the thief had to be either you or your cousin Willard. You're about the same size, and your voices are not unalike. The quickest way to be sure was to see who listened over our wiretapped telephone line. I realized someone was still listening because earlier today I made the mistake of calling Chief Reynolds on our phone and someone warned the window smasher."

"No proof?" Sarah Temple said, sounding stunned.

"Not until now," Jupiter admitted.

"Why, you . . . !" The girl grabbed a large hammer from a workbench and raised it toward Jupiter. "I . . . I'll—!"

All at once figures stood up around the outdoor workshop in the last light of the day. They were Chief Reynolds and his men with Bob and Pete and Paul. The tall Second Investigator stood a little shamefaced near the pile of lumber he had bumped into earlier, almost giving the trap away. One more person stood with the police and the boys. A bent figure who leaned on a cane as he limped slowly toward Sarah Temple. She still held the hammer raised to strike Jupiter.

"You will do nothing, young lady," Jarvis Temple said, no longer furious, only sad. "My own niece a thief. I blame myself. I made your life too easy, indulging all those whims—the car, the radio equipment, the electronics, the skiing, the mountain climbing. Always giving you the things you thought you had to have. I should have given you my attention instead. Well, perhaps it isn't too late." The old man sighed.

Chief Reynolds signaled one of his men to take Sarah Temple. The dark-haired girl looked at the policeman who held her. She uttered a cry of anger, broke loose, and reached into her pocket.

"If I can't have it, no one will!" She drew back her arm and threw, but as she did so, the policeman grabbed her elbow. The object in her hand flew straight up in the air and came down near Pete. He reached out and caught it.

He opened his hand. The round, golden coin gleamed as brightly as the Rolls-Royce even in the now dark night. Everyone stared at it wordlessly.

"I thought she might have it with her," Jupiter

said. "It is very hard to sell such a rare coin without attracting attention."

Chief Reynolds nodded once more to the patrolman holding Sarah Temple. The policeman touched her. She looked up at him, her eyes bewildered.

"But it was so easy," she said. "I needed so many things. The eagle was there in the car. Someone was smashing car windows all over town. It was going to be so easy."

20
Mr. Sebastian
Offers a Challenge

A few days later, Jupiter, Pete, and Bob sat in the gray panel truck in the driveway of the Jacobs' store. Paul, happily back behind the steering wheel, called to his dad outside.

"So it's okay if I drive the guys?"

"Wherever you like, Paul. I owe you that much for doubting you."

"It's okay, Dad. I can see how it looked to you."

"Imagine," Mr. Jacobs said, "a man on a bicycle breaking car windows so he could sell the glass to repair them! I would never have believed it! But you boys proved it, and I'm proud of Paul for his part in solving the mystery. Or should I say mysteries, considering the young lady copycat?"

"Yes," Jupiter agreed, "the mysteries really had

no connection beyond Sarah's imitating William
Margon and hoping he'd be blamed for everything."

"A frustrated hope, thanks to you boys," said Mr.
Jacobs, beaming.

Soon Paul was driving the panel truck up the Coast
Highway. Near Malibu, Pete told him to turn off into
Cypress Canyon Drive. They bumped along the side
road and stopped at a large white house with neon
strips around the eaves, the only clue to its former
identity as a restaurant. The boys piled out of the
truck and rang the front doorbell.

After a few moments of silence they heard the tap-
tap-tap of a cane approaching. The door was opened
by a thin man with graying hair. It was Hector
Sebastian, the Three Investigators' friend and men-
tor. A former private detective, Sebastian had turned
to writing mystery novels and screenplays when his
right leg was badly injured in an accident.

"Hello, boys," Sebastian said. "Come on in."

He led the way to the living room, leaning on his
cane, and seated the boys at the patio table in front
of the fireplace.

"Where's Don?" asked Jupe. Hoang Van Don, who
was Sebastian's Vietnamese houseman and cook, usually answered the door for his employer.

"He's busy," said Mr. Sebastian. "He's getting ready
to cook some treat for us."

The writer gestured toward the terrace that ran

the length of the glass-fronted living room, over-looking the Coast Highway and the Pacific Ocean. On the far end of the terrace sat a slim young man in a white shirt and black slacks. His legs were en-twined in the lotus position and his eyes stared va-cantly out over the ocean. His face wore a serene expression.

"Getting ready to cook?" said Bob. "He looks like he's meditating."

"He is," said Mr. Sebastian. "Don's become a fan of a new cooking program on cable TV. I call the chef the 'gourmet guru.' He advocates meditating before you start to work. Says it clears the mind and lets you concentrate better. He's quite right. I've begun meditating myself before I hit the word processor every day."

"I'm sure it helps," said Jupe. "But what kind of food does the guru advocate?" He shuddered slightly as he recalled some of the exotic health foods Don had served the Investigators on recent visits.

"Don't panic." The writer laughed. "The gourmet guru makes famous dishes from around the world. The food around here has improved tremendously.

"Now," continued the mystery writer, "tell me about your new case. The hints you gave me on the phone whetted my appetite."

"It all started with Paul Jacobs, here," said Jupiter, introducing the Investigators' new friend. Bob pulled out his notes on the case and handed them across the table to Sebastian.

The writer sat forward in his chair and started to read. While the boys waited, they saw Don stand up on the terrace and disappear around the side of the house. Soon faint sounds of doors closing and pots banging came from the kitchen.

Finally Sebastian put down Bob's notes and sat back.

"What a story. I'd never have believed William Margon's scheme if you hadn't proved it. Is he being punished?"

"Yes," Pete said. "His father is going to pay back everyone who had a window smashed, and the judge put William on probation for as long as it takes him to repay his father. He's been demoted to a yard worker at Margon until he earns a promotion by hard work. He won't be driving fancy cars or buying expensive clothes for a while."

"That should make him shape up," Mr. Sebastian said. "And what about Sarah Temple?"

"She's in for a hard time, too," Bob said. "Luckily, she hadn't sold the double eagle yet, so old Jarvis didn't press charges. But he's taken away her car, her radios, her electronics equipment, and everything else he bought her—and he's kicked her out of his house."

"Sounds like a cold man," Mr. Sebastian said. "He

was probably right to blame himself for much of her wrong thinking."

"Yes," Jupiter said, "but he's not really heartless. He's helping Sarah find a job at a radio station, where her talents will be valued, and he will continue to pay for her college courses in electronics. But aside from that, she's going to have to earn her own way."

"I guess she and William Margon have to learn the hard way," Mr. Sebastian said. "There's really no shortcut to success."

Jupiter suddenly noticed that a delicious aroma was wafting into the room. His mouth started to water as he wondered how long they'd have to wait for Don's gourmet treat. Suppressing a sigh, he listened to Hector Sebastian's next question.

"Jupe, after your confrontation with Sarah Temple, you said she might have gotten away with her theft— even after William's capture—except for one small error. What was that error?"

"She smashed the wrong window," Jupiter said. "As soon as I realized that, I knew we had a copycat crime. The coin had been left on the passenger's seat, so Sarah broke the window next to the curb. But as the window smasher rode past, he broke only the front windows on the driver's side. There was no way the biker could have shot out the curbside front window from the street!"

"A copycat who made a bad copy," Mr. Sebastian

said, and hurried on before the boys could groan at his joke. "One more point, Jupe. When you and Paul called the police from the salvage yard, you didn't know yet that the biker was William Margon. You only knew the biker worked at Margon Glass. So how did Sarah Temple, overhearing you on the wiretap, know whom to warn with her call to the company?"

Jupiter tore his attention away from the pungent aroma now filling the room and answered the mystery writer.

"She didn't. She simply called the company and described the biker to the person who answered the phone. As it happened, everyone at Margon Glass knew about William Margon and his bike riding, and her description fit no one else."

"So she was lucky," Mr. Sebastian said, "and so were you. If she hadn't called you would have had a much harder time identifying William and catching Sarah."

"But we would have done it," Bob said firmly.

"Probably," Mr. Sebastian said. "But let me tell you a secret I learned in my years as a private detective: A little luck can take you a long way. Hard work and a little luck can wrap up any case."

At that moment the door to the kitchen swung open at the other end of the room. Don came through it, proudly holding a tray before him. He advanced to the table and set down five small round tin plates and some odd utensils. There were six depressions in the metal of each plate. In each depression was a snail shell.

"Snails!" Don announced, beaming at the boys. "Traditional taste treat of French cuisine. Favorite of gourmet eaters around the world."

Appalled, the four boys gazed at the Vietnamese houseman. Fortunately he didn't notice. Hector Sebastian was busy complimenting him on the feast, and Don went back to the kitchen smiling.

Sebastian looked at the boys and chuckled. "No one can consider himself sophisticated if he doesn't appreciate snails," the writer informed them.

"Um, thanks just the same, but I'm not sure I'm ready to become sophisticated," said Jupe.

"Me, either," chorused the other boys.

"Oh, come on," said Sebastian. "Anyone brave enough to trap criminals is brave enough to try a snail. Now, here's how you eat them."

With his left hand, the writer grasped a snail shell with a clamplike utensil. His right hand twisted a small fork with two long tines deep into the shell. He pulled out a grayish, rubbery-looking blob covered with melted butter and minced parsley, and popped it into his mouth.

"Delicious!" he said. "Now you try it."

For a minute no one moved. Then Pete gingerly

picked up the utensils and extracted a snail. His friends held their breath as he chewed.

"Hey," he said, "it's not rubbery at all! It's soft. And all you taste is garlic butter. It's really pretty good!"

One by one the other boys tried a snail, but only Pete really liked them. He and Hector Sebastian finished what the others left on their plates.

Then the boys said goodbye and headed for the door.

"Whew!" said Jupe as they walked outside. "I'd rather trap a criminal any day!"

THE THREE INVESTIGATORS MYSTERY SERIES

The Secret of Terror Castle
The Mystery of the Stuttering Parrot
The Mystery of the Whispering Mummy
The Mystery of the Green Ghost
The Mystery of the Vanishing Treasure
The Secret of Skeleton Island
The Mystery of the Fiery Eye
The Mystery of the Silver Spider
The Mystery of the Screaming Clock
The Mystery of the Moaning Cave
The Mystery of the Talking Skull
The Mystery of the Laughing Shadow
The Secret of the Crooked Cat
The Mystery of the Coughing Dragon
The Mystery of the Flaming Footprints
The Mystery of the Nervous Lion
The Mystery of the Singing Serpent
The Mystery of the Shrinking House
The Secret of Phantom Lake
The Mystery of Monster Mountain
The Secret of the Haunted Mirror
The Mystery of the Dead Man's Riddle
The Mystery of the Invisible Dog
The Mystery of Death Trap Mine
The Mystery of the Dancing Devil
The Mystery of the Headless Horse
The Mystery of the Magic Circle
The Mystery of the Deadly Double
The Mystery of the Sinister Scarecrow
The Secret of Shark Reef
The Mystery of the Scar-Faced Beggar
The Mystery of the Blazing Clifs
The Mystery of the Purple Pirate
The Mystery of the Wandering Cave Man
The Mystery of the Kidnapped Whale
The Mystery of the Missing Mermaid
The Mystery of the Two-Toed Pigeon
The Mystery of the Smashing Glass
The Mystery of the Trail of Terror
and
The Three Investigators' Book of Mystery Puzzles

THE THREE INVESTIGATORS MYSTERY SERIES

NOVELS

The Secret of Terror Castle
The Mystery of the Stuttering Parrot
The Mystery of the Whispering Mummy
The Mystery of the Green Ghost
The Mystery of the Vanishing Treasure
The Secret of Skeleton Island
The Mystery of the Fiery Eye
The Mystery of the Silver Spider
The Mystery of the Screaming Clock
The Mystery of the Moaning Cave
The Mystery of the Talking Skull
The Mystery of the Laughing Shadow
The Secret of the Crooked Cat
The Mystery of the Coughing Dragon
The Mystery of the Flaming Footprints
The Mystery of the Nervous Lion
The Mystery of the Singing Serpent
The Mystery of the Shrinking House
The Secret of Phantom Lake
The Mystery of Monster Mountain
The Secret of the Haunted Mirror
The Mystery of the Dead Man's Riddle
The Mystery of the Invisible Dog
The Mystery of Death Trap Mine
The Mystery of the Dancing Devil
The Mystery of the Headless Horse
The Mystery of the Magic Circle
The Mystery of the Deadly Double
The Mystery of the Sinister Scarecrow
The Secret of Shark Reef
The Mystery of the Scar-Faced Beggar
The Mystery of the Blazing Cliffs
The Mystery of the Purple Pirate
The Mystery of the Wandering Cave Man
The Mystery of the Kidnapped Whale
The Mystery of the Missing Mermaid
The Mystery of the Two-Toed Pigeon
The Mystery of the Smashing Glass
The Mystery of the Trail of Terror
The Mystery of the Rogues' Reunion

(*Continued on next page*)

FIND YOUR FATE™ MYSTERIES

The Case of the Weeping Coffin
The Case of the Dancing Dinosaur

PUZZLE BOOKS

The Three Investigators' Book of Mystery Puzzles